MYSTERY OF THE LOST TREASURE

Presented to the library
in honor of

Sheila Reynolds - 12/14/70
Jeff Schrock - 12/17/70
and
Jeff Lengacher - 12/31/68

By the Primary Junior Department
1981-1982

MYSTERY OF THE LOST TREASURE

Ruth Nulton Moore

Illustrated by James L. Converse

HERALD PRESS
Scottdale, Pennsylvania
Kitchener, Ontario
1978

Library of Congress Cataloging in Publication Data

Moore, Ruth Nulton.
  Mystery of the lost treasure.

  SUMMARY: Two youngsters follow clues from an
old diary hoping to find a treasure buried years
ago on their aunt's Pennsylvania farm.
  [1. Buried treasure—Fiction. 2. Pennsylvania
—Fiction. 3. Mystery and detective stories]
I. Converse, James. II. Title.
PZ7.M7878My   [Fic]   78-11748
ISBN 0-8361-1870-7
ISBN 0-8361-1871-5 pbk.

MYSTERY OF THE LOST TREASURE
Copyright © 1978 by Herald Press, Scottdale, Pa.15683
    Kitchener, Ont N2G 4M5
Library of Congress Catalog Card Number: 78-11748
International Standard Book Numbers:
    0-8361-1870-7 (hardcover)
    0-8361-1871-5 (softcover)
Printed in the United States of America
Design: Alice B. Shetler

10 9 8 7 6 5 4 3 2 1

To
Bernice Hufford Moore
and the
memory of
Ralph Herman Moore
for their
generous and
cheerful
encouragement.

CONTENTS

1

A RUINED SUMMER

"THERE GOES my summer!" cried Joey Howard in a painful tone of voice. "Where's my team going to get another first baseman who's a lefty, I'd like to know!"

"Do we have to go?" wailed his sister Jan. "Patty Dawson and I have so many things planned for August."

Jan and Joey looked at one another woefully. They had the same round, freckled faces, the same sandy-colored hair, and the same bright blue eyes.

Anyone could tell at first glance that they were twins.

Their father and mother were sitting at the kitchen table across from them. Mr. Howard drew in a deep sigh as he glanced down at the letter he had spread out on the table. "Well, Aunt Melinda seems awfully anxious to have you two spend the month of August with her at White Meadow Farm."

"It does seem strange, though," Mrs. Howard put in, "that she would suddenly invite Jan and Joey to visit her this summer. Why, they hardly know her. They were too young to remember their visit to the farm seven years ago."

Mr. Howard frowned thoughtfully at the letter. "Well, maybe she thinks they should know more about the family homestead now that they're old enough to travel by themselves. White Meadow Farm has been in the Howard family for four generations. I used to spend my summers there when I was a boy and Grandpa and Grandma Howard were living. When they passed away, Aunt Melinda stayed on at the farm by herself."

"Aunt Melinda is our great-aunt, isn't she?" Jan asked.

Mr. Howard nodded.

"What was the farm like when you stayed there?" Joey wanted to know.

Mr. Howard thought for a moment, then a smile curved his mouth as he remembered the good times he had at White Meadow Farm when he was a boy. "Well, there was a barn and a big meadow filled with so many Queen Anne's lace that it looked

10

white. That's how the farm got the name White Meadow Farm. The meadow ran down to the shores of a lake where Grandpa and I used to fish. We caught lots of pickerel and bass in those days."

Mr. Howard paused and looked at the twins, his eyes twinkling. "It might be fun you know."

"But for a whole *month!*" protested Joey.

And Jan added, "Patty promised to let me swim in her new pool every day now that it's finished. We planned cookouts and sleep-outs and lots of neat things for August."

Mr. Howard's smile faded and he looked at the twins with serious gray eyes. "I know you'll be missing a lot of fun here, but by the sounds of this letter, Aunt Melinda will be terribly disappointed if you two don't visit her."

"It must be lonesome for her, living there by herself since Grandpa and Grandma Howard died," Mrs. Howard remarked. "Maybe she's thinking of selling the farm and wants the twins to visit it before she does."

Mr. Howard shook his head, "I can't imagine Aunt Melinda ever wanting to sell White Meadow Farm. As I said, it's been in the family for four generations and she dearly loves the old place."

They stopped talking and Jan studied her parents' faces for a long moment. She knew that neither Dad nor Mom would force her and Joey to go, but she also knew how much they wanted them to please Aunt Melinda. With a deep sigh, she said, "Well—maybe we should go if it would make Aunt Melinda feel good."

"I think it would be a great kindness to your

great-aunt if you did visit her this summer," Mrs. Howard said, reaching over and giving Jan's hand a little squeeze.

Joey still looked grimly determined not to go until his mother turned to him and asked, "What about it, Joey?"

He looked down at the table and traced the rose pattern on the place mat with his fingers. When Mom asked him in that tone of voice, what could he say? He knew his parents really wanted him to go, and after all, Jan was willing to give up her good times for the rest of the summer.

"Oh, okay," he conceded, "but just this one summer." Then with a deep sigh he added, "I suppose I'd better go tell the guys on the team that they'll just have to get another first baseman for August."

It took a great deal of planning and letters back and forth between the Howard's home in Ohio and Aunt Melinda's farm in eastern Pennsylvania before Jan and Joey were ready to leave. At last, on the first day of August, they waved goodbye to their parents in Columbus and were on their way. They changed buses in Pittsburgh, and for the rest of the long day they traveled across the endless Pennsylvania mountains.

It was night by the time they reached Scranton, the end of their journey. When they walked into the bus depot with their luggage, a spry little woman with gray hair and sparkling blue eyes hurried up to meet them. She walked with a brisk step that reminded the twins of the way their father walked. She wore a bright-colored summer dress, was

12

bareheaded, and carried a large plastic shopping bag on her arm.

"Janice and Joseph?" she called as she approached them anxiously.

The twins nodded, and she thrust out both hands to greet them. "I'm your Great-Aunt Melinda. My, how nice of you to come and visit me." She gave them both a hug and before they could say a word, she shepherded them to the nearest phone booth. "I promised your parents that I would call the minute you got off the bus. Maybe you'd like to talk with them, too, and tell them you arrived here safely."

After brief conversations with Mom and Dad, the twins followed Aunt Melinda from the bus station to an old black sedan in the parking lot.

"I know Bessie is an old relic, but she goes," their great-aunt assured them as she drew a set of car keys from the plastic shopping bag.

"How far is White Meadow Farm from here?" Jan asked when she had seated herself in the front seat next to Aunt Melinda. Joey got into the backseat with the luggage.

"Twenty miles," Aunt Melinda replied. "White Meadow Farm is in the heart of the Pocono Mountains. You'll like our mountains. Your father did when he was a boy."

Aunt Melinda turned the ignition key and the old car sputtered a moment. Then it bolted out of the parking lot. Joey clung to the backseat and wondered if Aunt Melinda knew how to drive the old relic.

They traveled through city streets then up a steep hill, leaving the city of Scranton behind them.

Joey gazed out the rear window at the long valley, sparkling with lights, until it disappeared below the dark mountain they were climbing.

"Pennsylvania sure is a lot different from Ohio," Jan remarked as the ancient car groaned up steep, wooded rises and swung around sharp, narrow curves. "I wish it were daylight so that we could see the mountains."

"You'll see enough mountains tomorrow," Aunt Melinda told her. "White Meadow Farm is right in the middle of them." Then she went on chattering about all the things their father did at the farm when he was their age and what good times they could have, too.

Alone in the backseat Joey thought gloomily, *Well, maybe Dad liked being miles away from home in these lonely mountains where there isn't even a streetlight, but he didn't belong to a first-place baseball team when he was twelve. In fact, Dad didn't even know how to play baseball nor did he know what it meant to a team to lose their best first baseman. Some vacation this is going to be!*

Aunt Melinda reached into the glove compartment and pulled out a bag of peppermints. "Here, Janice, help yourself and hand the bag back to Joseph."

"Aunt Melinda, everybody calls me Jan and Joseph, Joey," Jan informed her.

"Even your parents?"

"Um hm," Jan said, her mouth full of peppermint.

"Well, all right," their great-aunt replied, "then I will, too. People called me Milly when I was a girl."

14

She chuckled softly and grabbed the steering wheel tighter as they swung around a sharp curve and bounced over some rocks. At first the twins thought the old car had gone off the road, but by the glow from the headlights they could see that they had turned off the highway and were now traveling along a narrow, stony, country road.

"We'll soon be there," Aunt Melinda announced as she shifted gears. "This is the road that leads to the lake."

"It sure is dark," Jan murmured. Everything was pitch black except the little square of road the car lights shone on. There were no streetlights and no house lights to brighten up the lonely road. There were only the tiny, distant stars that pierced through the dark sky above them.

"Don't you ever get lonely living way back here all by yourself, Aunt Melinda?"

"Landsakes, child, I've been living here all my life. Wouldn't know how to act, living anywhere else."

Jan thought she caught something a little odd in Aunt Melinda's voice when she said this, but her great-aunt quickly changed the subject and her voice was cheerful again. "There's a surprise out in the barn that I'm sure you two will like. You can find out what it is tomorrow."

It's probably another old relic like this car, Joey thought grimly.

Aunt Melinda turned the car into a narrow lane and brought it to a halt by a large farmhouse built of gray fieldstone. They all clambered out.

"I'll put Bessie in the garage tomorrow," Aunt

15

Melinda told them. "It's late and we have your luggage to take in."

She fumbled for her door key in the dark, found the keyhole, and swung open a squeaky screen door. "Always come in by way of the kitchen," she told the twins. "It's handy that way."

A fury of barks greeted them as they stepped into the dark house. Aunt Melinda found the wall switch and soon the room was flooded with light.

The children blinked their eyes in the sudden brightness. From an old rag rug in front of the stove a black cocker spaniel rushed over to them. He wiggled all over, his tail going a mile-a-minute.

"Calm down, Inky," Aunt Melinda scolded.

Jan leaned over to pat the frisky little dog. He was black from his nose to the tip of his wagging tail. *Inky's a good name for him,* she thought.

Aunt Melinda drew a box of dog biscuits from her shopping bag and rattled it. "See what I brought for you from town."

Inky stopped barking and sniffed at the box. Then he sat up on his two hind legs and waved his two front paws in the air. "Ruff, ruff," he barked as if he were saying, "Thank you."

The twins laughed and Aunt Melinda motioned for them to sit down.

"Now for a nice cool drink of lemonade before bed," she said, pushing back a wisp of gray hair and tucking it into the bun in back of her head.

Jan seated herself in a low rocker and looked about her while Aunt Melinda fussed at the sink with glasses and ice cubes. The kitchen was the largest one she had ever seen. There were two other

16

rocking chairs by the windows and an old corner cupboard was tucked away in one corner. A gas stove stood along one wall, hiding a boarded-up fireplace from long ago. An embroidered copy of the Lord's Prayer in a huge gilded frame hung on the opposite wall. Wide windowsills, holding potted begonias and African violets, brightened the large black windowpanes.

As she rocked slowly, Jan went miles away in her mind, back home to Ohio where her and Patty's parents were probably chatting together from their patios. A wave of homesickness rushed over her at that moment and she felt a sudden lump rise in her throat. Everything was so strange and quiet in this lonely place that she wondered how she and Joey would ever be able to stand it here for an entire month.

She looked up to find Aunt Melinda's smiling face meeting hers over a tray of frosty lemonade glasses. Jan took a glass and forced a smile back at her great-aunt.

They sat quietly rocking and sipping their cold drinks. The slow ticking of the kitchen clock on the mantle above the hearth made Jan feel sleepy. It had been a long day and seemed ages ago since they had left Ohio.

Aunt Melinda glanced at the clock. "Mercy, I didn't know it was so late! You children must be tired after such a long trip. Put the glasses in the sink and I'll help you with your suitcases and show you your rooms."

She led the way through a dark, high-ceilinged parlor then up a long flight of stairs. At the top the

17

twins followed her along a hallway past a row of bedrooms on either side. *If each door had a number on it,* Jan thought, *it would seem like a small hotel.*

In the middle of the hall, Aunt Melinda opened the two bedroom doors across from each other. She pointed out Joey's room to him and led Jan into hers.

Jan put her suitcase on the bed and looked about the room. There was a tall walnut wardrobe in one corner and a chest of drawers in the other. Two faded rag rugs covered the wide floor boards and on the bed was an old-fashioned quilt of many colors. An oval-framed portrait of a girl in a high-buttoned, lacy dress hung over the bed.

"I thought you'd like this room," Aunt Melinda said when she noticed Jan looking at the portrait. "It belonged to your great-great-grandmother, Martha Howard, when she was a girl your age and lived here."

After Aunt Melinda was satisfied that Jan was settled, she kissed her good-night and hurried across the hall to Joey's room. Jan unpacked her suitcase and hung her clothes in the wardrobe. She slipped out of her shoes and got into bed.

From where she lay, she could look up and see the portrait of her great-great-grandmother smiling down at her. The smile seemed strange and mysterious—as strange and mysterious as this old house.

Jan shivered and snuggled farther down into her covers. She felt better after she had said her prayers. She turned off the little table lamp by her bed and began to think about the surprise in the barn that their great-aunt had mentioned.

I wonder what it can be, she told herself just before she dropped off to sleep. She just couldn't imagine.

She was still wondering about the surprise when she awoke the next morning. After making her bed and dressing in a pair of jeans and a blouse, she went across the hall to her brother's room.

She knocked at the door and called, "Are you awake, Joey?"

When there was no answer, she opened the door and peered into the room. Joey was a dark, silent mound, curled up in the middle of an old iron bed.

"Come on, Sleepyhead, get up," Jan said, shaking his shoulder. With a groan Joey opened his eyes.

"Where are we?" he asked in a thick, sleepy voice. He propped himself up on one elbow and blinked his eyes at the strange room.

"We're at Aunt Melinda's, silly," Jan told him.

"Oh, oh—yeah," Joey said, pushing back his covers and swinging his legs out of bed.

"Come on, get dressed. I'll wait for you on the stair landing."

A few minutes later Joey sprinted out of his room and they went down stairs together. In the kitchen Aunt Melinda was getting breakfast. She darted about cheerfully with the quickness of a small gray wren.

"I thought you two would never get up," she greeted them. "How do you like your eggs? Sunnyside up?"

"That would be fine, thank you," Jan said politely.

19

While they ate breakfast, Inky sat by the table and begged with his eyes. Jan fed him some bacon and Joey made him sit up and beg for a piece of toast.

"He's quite a beggar," Aunt Melinda said, laughing. "Likes table food better than his own."

After they had eaten and had helped Aunt Melinda with the dishes, Jan asked eagerly, "May we go to the barn and see what the surprise is?"

"Why, of course you may," replied Aunt Melinda. "I'm going to feed the chickens and gather the eggs. You may come with me and I'll show you where the stable is. The surprise is there."

She went into the pantry for the egg basket and then they were ready to leave. Jan opened the screen door and the little cocker spaniel leaped outside ahead of them. The morning was warm and hazy blue as August mornings usually are. Across the yard from the house they spied the barn, its boards weathered gray through the years. Beyond the barn was a large meadow that stretched down to the lake, and as Dad had said, the meadow was white with Queen Anne's lace.

Along one side of the barn was a chicken house, filled with squawking white hens, and on the other side was a small building that looked like a toolshed. Before Aunt Melinda went into the chicken house, she pointed out the stable underneath the main part of the barn.

"That's where you'll find the surprise," she told them, her blue eyes twinkling.

They climbed the fence that enclosed the barnyard and walked across to the stable door. Jan

20

reached it first. The top part of the stable door was open. Standing on tiptoes, she peered inside.

It didn't take long to discover what Aunt Melinda's surprise was. She caught her breath then squealed with delight, "Oh, Joey, look—a horse!"

2

THE DIARY

JAN SLAPPED the reins against the little horse's neck and galloped hard along the dusty road that skirted White Meadow Lake. Black threatening clouds were sweeping across the lake that made the water look gray and angry. Thunder began to rumble behind the hill of pines alongside the meadow.

Jan was thankful now that she and Joey had begged their parents to take riding lessons last year and that they had learned to ride so well. They had even learned how to bridle and saddle a horse and how to brush and curry it after riding. But not one of the horses at the riding academy could compare with the little quarter horse she and Joey had found in Aunt Melinda's barn.

What a surprise it was! After they had found the horse, they dashed into the chicken house to ask Aunt Melinda about it.

Aunt Melinda was bending over the straw nests along the back wall. "Shut the door so the hens don't get out," she had called quickly over her shoulder. Then she told them that she was boarding the horse for a family who had a cottage across the lake.

"The McNeils come to the lake mostly on weekends and have to have someone care for Patches when they aren't here," Aunt Melinda had explained, handing Jan a smooth white egg that was still warm. "Since I have an empty stable in my barn, I offered to board their horse."

Aunt Melinda straightened up and looked wistful. "It's good to have a horse in that stable again after so many years."

After Jan and Joey had helped gather the rest of the eggs and had assured Aunt Melinda that they could both ride well, she let them bridle and saddle Patches and take turns riding on the road along the lake. "There's hardly any traffic on this side of the lake," she told them, "and the McNeils said it would be all right for you to ride Patches. The exercise will do her good."

Now as Jan came to the lane leading into White Meadow Farm, she urged the little horse to go

23

faster. "Come on, Patches, we'll soon be home," she called above the rising wind.

Patches galloped at full speed straight toward her stable in the old barn. Joey had the barnyard gate open and was waiting for them.

"Hurry up," he shouted when he saw them coming. Jan reined in the horse and slid down from the saddle. Joey grabbed the reins and led Patches into the stable. Jan came running after them and drew the stable door shut just as the first big drop of rain splashed down on top of her head.

"Whew, that was close," she gasped. "Mountain storms sure do come up fast."

Joey led the horse to her stall. "We better get her rubbed down. She's all sweaty from galloping so hard." He threw an admiring glance at his sister. "You sure can ride, Janny."

Jan patted the little quarter horse's flanks. "For a horse, Patches sure can gallop."

Patches was a pinto and her coat was made up of red and white markings that looked just like red and white patches, which probably had given her her name. The twins got busy at once with currycomb and brush. Patches stood perfectly still and blew contentedly through her nostrils, enjoying the rubbing down she was getting after the hard ride.

When they were finished, Joey hung the saddle on a wooden saddle horse and Jan filled the pinto's feedbox with oats. Then they opened the top part of the stable door and looked out. The storm had settled down to steady rain. Big drops dripped from the eaves of the old barn, forming little pools of muddy water in the barnyard. The pines on the other side of the meadow were veiled in gray mist and the lake was hidden from view.

"I guess that's the end of our riding for today." Jan said ruefully. "Now what can we do?" She looked questioningly at her brother.

"We could explore the rest of the barn," Joey suggested, glancing back at the dark wooden steps that led up to the threshing floor and the haylofts above.

Jan shook her head. "It's too dark and scary up there on a day like this. Let's save that for a sunny day and play in the house instead."

"Okay," Joey agreed reluctantly, "but I don't know what we can do in the house. Aunt Melinda doesn't even have a TV."

They gave Patches a parting pat and made a dash between the raindrops for the stone farmhouse.

Aunt Melinda was whipping up a batter of gingerbread when they came bursting into the kitchen.

"Umm," murmured Joey as he peered into the bowl of rich brown batter.

"When the gingerbread is done, I'll call you," Aunt Melinda said, laughing.

"You won't have to call twice," Joey told her.

Jan walked over to the window and watched the raindrops streaming down the pane. "It *would* have to rain our first day here," she said with a sigh.

"Yeah, what's there to do now?" Joey was remembering the favorite TV programs he liked to watch on rainy days at home.

"Well," Aunt Melinda said, "you could do what your father used to do here on rainy days. You could play in the secret room in the attic."

Jan swung around from the window and stared

at her great-aunt with surprise. "A secret room?"

There was a sparkle in Aunt Melinda's eyes as she poured the batter into two cake pans. "Didn't you know my attic has a secret room?"

The twins shook their heads.

"It's a good place to play on a rainy day," their great-aunt continued. "My, the good times your father had up there and me, too, when I was a girl. That's where my mother put the big trunk packed with old clothes. I used to enjoy dressing up in those old hats and dresses."

"Sounds like fun," Jan said, her eyes lighting up.

"It is fun," Aunt Melinda told her. "Why don't you and Joey see if you can find that secret room?"

"Is it hard to find?"

"Not too hard. Your father found it when he was your age."

"Well, if Dad could find it, I guess we can," Jan said giggling. "Mom says he can never find any- thing around the house."

"Well, he found the secret room."

"Then we can find it, too!" exclaimed Joey. "Come on, Jan, let's go."

Not intending to be left behind, Inky leaped up from his rug by the stove and followed them through the parlor to the front hallway.

"The door to the attic is the first one at the top of the stairs," Aunt Melinda called after them.

The twins took the stairs two steps at a time. Joey reached the top first. "This must be the door."

"Well, open it," Jan said impatiently.

Joey lifted the old-fashioned latch and the attic door squeaked open slowly. In back of it they glimpsed a narrow, winding stairway that circled upward to the mysterious gloom above.

"You go first," Jan said.

Joey climbed the steps slowly, with Jan and Inky following close behind. At the top they paused and looked around them curiously. Queer shapes loomed up all around them, black and foreboding, until Joey made his way across the attic and raised the blinds on the windows to let the daylight in. Then the shapes took the forms of boxes of all sizes and old furniture. There was a hatstand with hats still hanging on its pegs, an old spinning wheel tucked away in the corner, and an ancient wash-stand with a stuffed owl perched on top of it.

Joey walked over to examine the stuffed owl. "Wow, look at this, will you! There's sure a lot of old stuff up here."

"Well, what did you expect?" Jan told him. "This attic holds four generations of old things, so it's bound to be cluttered." She peered into a dark, cob-webby corner. "I wonder why a secret room was built up here?"

"I'd like to know how we can find it," Joey said.

There were so many recesses and shadowy corners in the big attic that they didn't know where to search first for the secret room.

"Let's start knocking on the walls," Jan suggested. "I read in a mystery story once about someone doing that. When the wall sounded hollow, there was a hidden place behind it."

"Okay," Joey said, "we might as well start here at this end first."

Inky cocked his head inquisitively as they spent

the next several minutes knocking on the walls and listening for a hollow sound. He watched them for a while, then with a sharp bark he ran to the other end of the attic and began scratching on the wall.

Jan laughed. "Silly dog. Look, Joey, he's trying to help us."

They continued their search, thumping on the wall boards and listening for hollow sounds. Before they were half way around the attic, their knuckles began to ache. Jan stopped knocking and looked down at her red hands. "I don't think I can knock my way around this whole attic," she said.

Joey slumped down on the floor beside her. "Neither can I," he admitted. He looked across the attic to where the cocker spaniel was now lying, half asleep. When the dog saw Joey watching him, he perked up his ears and got to his feet. With a whine he started scratching on the far wall again.

Joey studied Inky with a puzzled frown. The little dog sure was acting queer. Then his tired face brightened. "Hey, you know what?" he told his sister. "Maybe Inky's helping more than you think. Maybe he's been up here before with Aunt Melinda when she went into the secret room for something. Maybe he knows where it is and is trying to tell us."

"Do you really think so?"

"Well, let's find out."

They scrambled to their feet and hurried across the attice to the far wall. Forgetting about their bruised knuckles, they began to knock on the wall where Inky had been scratching.

"This wall does sound hollow!" Jan cried excitedly.

"Then the secret room must be behind it," Joey exclaimed, "but how can we get into it?"

"We'll have to find the opening," Jan said. "It must be hidden somewhere in these panels."

"Maybe there's a hidden spring or something." Joey was really excited now. "You start at this end and I'll start over there."

They ran to opposite ends of the wall and started pushing against the panels, hoping that one would slide open, the way secret panels are supposed to. Slowly they made their way toward the middle where Inky stood watching them. Nothing happened.

"Rats, now what do we do?" asked Joey despairingly.

"We could ask Aunt Melinda," Jan suggested.

Joey shook his head stubbornly. "If Dad found the secret room when he was our age then we ought to be able to. After all, there are two of us."

With a sigh Jan leaned her weary shoulder heavily against the panel right above Inky's head. There was a soft click and she felt something move.

"Oh!" she whispered urgently. "The wall—it moved!"

The next moment she almost fell over backward as the middle panel began to swing inward then up, up until it was flat against the ceiling.

Joey leaped back. "Wow! We found it!"

"Ruff! Ruff!" barked Inky as if he were saying, "I told you so!"

Both children stared at the opening in the wall then up at the open panel. It was like a large trapdoor in the wall. When you pressed against it, a heavy spring released and drew it back against the ceiling. On the inner side of the panel, hidden from view, were the hinges and a long rope.

Joey looked up at the rope. "I wonder—" he mused, studying it for a moment. "Watch out, Jan. I'm going to see what happens."

He pulled on the rope and the long panel began to swing downward from the ceiling and into place again against the wall.

"That's how you close it," Joey said with an air of authority.

"Let's open it again," Jan said, pressing against the panel. Again it moved backward and then up against the ceiling.

Joey bent over and ruffled the cocker spaniel's long, silky ears. "Inky, old boy, thanks for showing us the secret room." Inky opened his mouth, his tongue lolling out in a wide smile.

Jan peered into the opening. "I can see the back wall over there where part of the chimney goes up through the roof."

They stepped inside the little room and looked around them. An old cot was placed against the chimney and next to it was a small table with a candle on it. The only other furniture was a chair in the corner and a large trunk right inside the door.

Jan bent over to examine the trunk. Bands of wood fastened with bright brass nailheads bound the sides of the trunk and its rounded top. This must be the trunk filled with old clothes that Aunt

"Can you imagine anybody wearing shoes like these?" Joey asked. "You'd have to have pointed toes to get into them."

30

Melinda had referred to. Eager to see what was inside, she opened the oval lid.

Joey wiggled his nose at the acrid smell of mothballs. "Just a lot of old clothes in here," he grumbled.

But Jan gave a squeal of delight as she reached down into the trunk and rummaged through its contents. "Oh, I think they're wonderful!" she exclaimed, drawing out a floppy old hat wreathed with long ostrich plumes. She tried it on and stepped out of the secret room to peer at herself in front of a big mirror.

Joey leaned over the trunk and pulled out a pair of shoes with funny, long-pointed toes. "Wow, look at these, will you!" he said holding up the shoes. "Can you imagine anybody wearing shoes like these? You'd have to have pointed toes to get into them."

"They're high-buttoned shoes, silly," Jan told him. "I'll bet Great-Great-Grandmother Howard wore these shoes when she was young."

"Weird!" Joey made a face and put the shoes back in the trunk.

Jan gave another squeal of delight as she drew out a long fur cape. She draped it around her shoulders. "Don't I look gorgeous?" she crowed as she walked around the trunk.

"Humph!" Joey retorted.

Jan strutted right in front of him with the cape dragging on the floor. Forgetting how long it was, she tripped over the end of it. Down she went amid hoots of laughter from Joey.

Rubbing her knee, she got up and glared at her

brother. This was one of the times she wished she had a twin sister instead of a twin brother. A sister wouldn't laugh at her all the time. A sister would like to play dress-up. All Joey wanted to do was to play his old baseball!

Joey ignored his sister's dark looks and plunged his arm down deep inside the trunk as far as it would go. Maybe there was something better than old clothes and high-buttoned shoes at the very bottom. His exploring fingers slipped past fur and silk and feathers until they touched something smooth and hard. He wriggled his fingertips around it. It felt like a small flat box. With a tumble of old hats and dresses he drew it out and sat back on his heels to examine it.

"Look what I found," he said.

Jan laid the cape and plumed hat aside and squatted down beside him.

"Open it," she said eagerly. "Let's see what's inside."

Joey tugged at the piece of faded blue ribbon tied around the box. The ribbon was so old that it tore as he tried to get the knot loose. With eager fingers, he opened the box and there lay an old leather-bound book.

Jan peered over his shoulder so close that he cried, "Hey, stop breathing down my neck, will you?"

"But I want to see, too," she wailed.

"Okay. Let's take it over to the window where there'll be more light."

After they had settled themselves in front of one of the little attic windows, Joey opened the book.

33

On the first page, in gilt letters, were printed the words: *My Diary.*

Jan's eyes danced with excitement. "An old diary!"

"Maybe this belonged to our great-great-great-grandfather Howard," Joey said as he turned to the first page. But when he saw the name that was written there, he gave a disappointed groan. The name, in frail, spidery letters, read: Martha Howard, and the date under the name was 1900.

Joey leafed impatiently through the stiff, crinkly pages, yellowed with age. "Probably full of dull, everyday happenings," he grumbled.

The faded brown ink was hard to read but they could make out some of it. Here was an account of the weather and a description of Martha Howard's new quilt she was making. Another page told of a visit to a new neighbor who had moved into a farm down the road. Joey flipped through more pages. There didn't seem to be anything exciting written on any of them that he could see, so he tossed the diary into Jan's lap.

"Here, you can have it, Janny. I'm going to look around the attic some more."

He walked over to the stuffed owl again then examined an assortment of shadowy objects against the wall. After a while he called out, "Boy, look what I found!" He held up several old fishing poles with the lines tangled around them. "If I can untangle these lines, I'll bet I could use them to go fishing. Maybe they're the ones Dad and Grandpa used when they went fishing on the lake."

Jan bent over the diary and neither one of them

spoke for a long time. The old attic was still except for the quiet drumming of raindrops on the eaves and the wind humming softly around the bricks in the chimney.

Joey had just finished untangling the last line when Jan's shrill voice rang out, "Come here, Joey. I really found something!"

"Probably a recipe for apple dumplings," Joey muttered, but he walked over to the window just the same.

Jan held out the old diary. "Read this," she demanded excitedly, thrusting the little book under her twin's nose.

Joey squinted down at the old-fashioned, squiggly handwriting. He studied the words in brown faded ink that Jan was pointing to. He made out the words "hidden" and "tunnel" and "under the farm." But what really made him catch his breath were the words "chest of gold" that leaped out of the page in front of him.

3
AUNT MELINDA'S STORY

"DOES IT really say 'chest of gold?' " cried Joey as he blinked down at the faded brown writing in the diary.

"It sure does," Jan said, jittery with excitement.

Joey squinted down at the rest of the page, then he pushed the diary toward his sister. "You read it," he said. "I can't figure out all those squiggles and you're a much better reader than I."

"The words are hard to make out," Jan admitted. "I guess that's how they wrote in those days." She held the diary close to the window and read slowly, " 'Elias Henry, the runaway slave my father and Mr. Sterret helped many years ago, has sent us a chest of gold coins which Papa put in the hidden tunnel under the farm for safekeeping. He said it would be safe in the tunnel with a ghost to guard it.' "

She stopped reading and blinked up at her brother. Joey was so excited that he almost fell over backward.

"A hidden tunnel, a chest of gold, and a ghost right here at White Meadow Farm!" he shouted. "Wow-ee! Let's hunt for that chest of gold, Janny. Let's see if we can find it!"

Jan's eyes turned suddenly serious. Unlike her impulsive twin who was ready that very minute to rush out and start searching for the chest of gold, she liked to think things out first before taking action.

"The gold was probably found a long time ago," she mused.

But Joey's hopes were not to be dimmed by what his sister had said. "And maybe it wasn't found, either," he challenged.

"Well, even if it wasn't found, the diary says a ghost guards it," Jan added with a shiver.

"Oh, pooh!" Joey said scornfully. "Nobody believes in ghosts these days."

Jan leafed back through the old book to see if she could find any mention of the mysterious ghost. She turned the crinkly old pages then stopped and drew in her breath sharply.

"Did you find something else?" asked Joey.

37

Jan didn't seem to hear him, she was so engrossed in what she was reading.

"Hey, let me see," Joey cried, making a grab for the diary.

Jan looked up and her voice quavered when she next spoke. "Joey, there is a ghost at White Meadow Farm and it has a name!"

Joey crowded close to his sister and peered down at the spidery writing. "Read it," he demanded impatiently.

Jan cleared her throat and read, " 'Last night there was a terrible storm and I saw the light again. It was moving across the meadow and disappeared into the barn. It was the ghost of Amos Brown returning to the tunnel!' "

Jan stopped reading and Joey asked, "Isn't there any more?"

Jan shook her head. "No, that's all that's written about it."

Joey leaned back, his blue eyes mystified. "Well, who was this Amos Brown, anyway, and why was his ghost returning to the tunnel?"

"And why was there a tunnel built under White Meadow Farm?" Jan added with a baffled look.

"Yeah, and what was Elias Henry, a runaway slave, doing here?"

With a puzzled shake of her head, Jan closed the diary. "We have a lot of answers to find," she said. "Let's ask Aunt Melinda. Maybe she'll know."

"Let's take the diary to the kitchen and ask her right now," Joey agreed.

The twins scrambled to their feet and raced down the attic stairs, Inky loping after them. When they reached the landing the delicious smell of gingerbread rose from the kitchen below. But the children were too excited about what they had found in the diary to think about gingerbread now.

Aunt Melinda heard them coming and when they reached the kitchen, she said, "You'll have to wait until the gingerbread is cool enough to cut." She paused a moment to stare at the old leather-bound diary Jan was holding. "So you found the secret room!" she said, sitting down in a rocker. "I see you found Martha Howard's diary, too."

"Then you know about the diary and the hidden tunnel and the chest of gold and the ghost?" asked Jan all in one breath.

"Of course I know about them," Aunt Melinda replied. "All the Howards have read that old diary. It has been in the trunk all these years."

Joey ran his fingers through his hair and looked puzzled. "But Dad never told us about it. He never said anything about the gold or the ghost."

"He probably didn't tell you because the gold has never been found and none of us has ever seen the ghost."

Joey swung around to his sister, his eyes round with excitement. "See, Janny, I told you that that chest of gold might not have been found!" Then he grinned. "Guarded by a ghost! Aunt Melinda said she never saw the ghost."

Jan looked down at the old diary with a puzzled frown. "But Martha Howard wrote that a ghost guards the treasure and it even has a name. Amos Brown. Who was Amos Brown, Aunt Melinda?"

Their great-aunt smiled mysteriously. "Well, I

39

see I have two curious children who want some answers," she said, getting up and walking over to the refrigerator. "Let's have lunch first, then I'll tell you all about it. What do you say we light a fire in the parlor grate and roast some wieners? It's a good day for an indoor picnic. We can have the gingerbread for dessert."

"Hey, that'll be fun," Joey said. "Can I build the fire, Aunt Melinda? I learned how to build cooking fires at summer camp last year."

"All right, Joey. You'll find some wood in the cellar. Jan and I will get the food ready."

A half hour later they were sitting in the parlor before the grate, toasting their weiners. The bright little fire in the black marble fireplace made the gray, gloomy day seem more cheerful. It even made the stiff Victorian parlor, with its dark paneled walls and heavy antique furniture, seem cozy.

Joey impatiently nudged his sister to hurry up and finish her gingerbread so that Aunt Melinda would tell them about all the mysterious and exciting things they had read in the diary. When Jan had nibbled the last crumb, he said eagerly, "Now will you tell about the hidden tunnel and the chest of gold and the ghost, Aunt Melinda?"

Aunt Melinda set her teacup on the table by her chair and reached for the diary Jan had brought into the parlor. She opened the old book and leafed through its pages for a moment before she answered. Then, leaning back in her chair, she said, "Maybe I had better start with the hidden tunnel first. Your great-great-great-grandfather, John Howard, had the tunnel built to connect the barn with the house. The house was built in 1858, just before the Civil War, and was a station in the Underground Railway."

"Underground Railway?" asked Joey, puzzled.

"Not a real railway, Joey," Aunt Melinda explained. "It was a way to hide runaway slaves on their journey to Canada where they would be free. You see, just before the Civil War, and during it, many slaves in the South escaped from their cruel masters. Along the way north to Canada they needed hiding places so that the slave hunters wouldn't find them. Here and there on their long journey they were hidden in secret places by people who did not believe in slavery and who wanted to help them. These secret places were called stations in the Underground Railway. Our White Meadow Farm was a station."

Joey's eyes were full of excitement. "Wow! It was?"

Aunt Melinda nodded and went on with her story. "The runaway slaves were brought to the barn then taken through the hidden tunnel to the house where John Howard hid them in the secret room. If anybody would have seen them enter the barn and searched it, they would not have found the runaways there because of the hidden tunnel. And if the slave hunters searched the house, they would not have been found here, either, because they were safe in the secret room in the attic."

"So that's why the secret room was built!" Jan exclaimed.

"Yes, that's the reason," Aunt Melinda answered. "John Howard had a false wall built in the attic on

41

the south side of the house so that from both the outside and the inside of the house, you couldn't tell that there was a room there at all."

"Were many runaway slaves hidden in the secret room?" Joey wanted to know.

"Yes, quite a few were brought here. They stayed in the secret room until John Howard got word that it was safe to move them on to the next station. Then, at night, he would row them across the lake where Henry Sterret, a man who lived on a farm on the other side, would meet them and guide them through the woods to the next station."

"Did the slave hunters ever catch any of the runaways?" Joey asked. He was sitting on the edge of his chair now. He had no idea that such exciting things had happened right here at this old farm.

"One slave didn't get away," Aunt Melinda replied, lowering her voice. "I remember your great-great-grandmother, Martha Howard, telling us about it when she was very old."

Aunt Melinda glanced down at the diary on her lap. "She wrote this diary, you know. Well, one night shortly after her father had hidden a man named Amos Brown, his master arrived with the sheriff. They were sure they had tracked the slave to our farm and stayed around for about a week looking for Amos. Even though they never found the hidden tunnel nor the secret room, they were still certain that Amos was here. However, poor Amos Brown was anxious to move on. It was terrible having to say cooped up in that small room in the attic for so long. He asked John Howard why he couldn't move to the next station. When your great-

great-great-grandfather told him about the danger, the poor man got more desperate than ever.

"One night when everybody was asleep in the house, Amos left the secret room in the attic and made his way through the tunnel and across the meadow to the lake where he hoped to find the boat that would take him across to Henry Sterret's farm. It was a dark and stormy night so Amos had to take a small lantern to guide his way across the meadow. He had almost reached the lake when a shot rang out. The sheriff, who had been promised a large reward from Amos' master, had been watching the farm day and night. When he saw Amos' light, he fired his gun in the air. When Amos didn't stop, he fired again. Poor Amos lost his head and started back across the meadow for the safety of the tunnel. The sheriff's bullet found him just as he was about to enter the barn. He died shortly after that inside the stable."

"Amos Brown is the name of the ghost in the diary," Jan said softly.

Aunt Melinda glanced down at the diary in her lap. "Yes, that's the name of the ghost. Mountain folks were superstitious in those days, and for many years after that they would say that on stormy nights a light would appear in our meadow, moving up toward the barn."

"Martha Howard saw it," Jan said again. "She wrote in her diary that she saw the ghost on a stormy night."

Aunt Melinda shook her head and reached for her cup of tea. "I suppose if you believe enough in ghosts, you can imagine you see them. Perhaps

Martha Howard did imagine that she saw a flickering light one stormy night in the meadow. Or it could have been a flash of lightning or somebody with a lantern and she thought it was the ghost."

When Jan still looked doubtful, Aunt Melinda said, "In all my years of living here, I have never seen the ghost, Jan. Of course," she added with a smile, "I've never looked for it either."

"What about the chest of gold?" Joey was more interested in the treasure at this moment than in the ghost.

Aunt Melinda took a sip of tea then replaced her cup on the table. "That concerns another runaway slave by the name of Elias Henry, who had a much happier ending. Elias Henry was the last runaway John Howard and Henry Sterret helped to freedom, and he never forget what they had done for him. Many years after the Civil War he sent a chest filled with gold coins to them as a gift for their kindness. You can imagine how surprised they were when they opened the chest and saw all the gold. There was a note in the chest written by Elias Henry, telling how he had accompanied a prospector who had mined for gold in the Yukon Territory in Northern Canada. The prospector had found a rich vein of ore and because Elias had shared the hardships of the Yukon winter with him, the prospector gave him half the gold. And in turn, Elias Henry shared his fortune with John Howard and Henry Sterret."

"That's a wonderful story," Jan said with a happy sigh, "but why wasn't the chest of gold ever found?"

Aunt Melinda bent over to poke at the fire. "That's been a mystery all these years," she told them. "The gold that belonged to our family and the Sterrets was put in the hidden tunnel for safekeeping. But since the time Martha Howard wrote about it in her diary that July day in 1900, not another thing has been mentioned about it. Shortly after the chest of gold was hidden, the Sterrets sold their farm and moved away. They were never heard from again, and a month after they had moved, John Howard died of a sudden stroke.

"He and Henry Sterret were the only two who knew where in the tunnel the treasure was hidden. They had told nobody else, not even their families, for fear that word would get out about the gold and it might be stolen. After John Howard's death, the family searched the hidden tunnel from top to bottom but were not able to find the treasure anywhere. It just seemed to have disappeared mysteriously."

"Henry Sterret knew where the gold was hidden," Jan put in. "Couldn't anybody find out where the Sterrets moved to?"

Aunt Melinda shook her head. "The Howards tried to locate Henry Sterret and his family, but nobody knew where they went after they left here, and none of the Sterrets has ever returned to White Meadow Lake—not even for their share of the gold."

"That sure is strange," Jan puzzled.

"Well, since nobody has ever found the gold, it must still be hidden somewhere in the tunnel," Joey reasoned. "It just has to be there!"

"It would seem that way," Aunt Melinda said. "That's why for generations our family has searched the tunnel for it. But nobody has been able to find it."

"That sure is a mystery," Joey said, shaking his head. "Can we hunt for the gold, Aunt Melinda?"

"I don't see why not. But don't be disappointed if you can't find it."

Aunt Melinda sat back in her chair and smiled at both of them. "I'm glad you know the secrets of our White Meadow Farm, and I'm glad you're here for part of your summer vacation. It's good for children to spend some time in the home that their ancestors built and lived in. I have lived in this old house all my life. It would seem strange to have to live anywhere else."

Jan thought she noticed little worry lines begin to form around Aunt Melinda's eyes when she said this. An expression—was it sadness or fear—flitted across her face.

Jan smiled up at her great-aunt. "It's fun being here with you, Aunt Melinda," she said. And she wasn't just saying this to make Aunt Melinda feel happy. She really meant it.

4

STEALTHY FOOTSTEPS

AFTER THEY had helped Aunt Melinda clear away the lunch, Joey said, "Let's start hunting for the lost treasure."

Jan's eyes brightened at the thought. "How can we find the hidden tunnel, Aunt Melinda?"

Their great-aunt was about to tell them when, at that very moment, there was a loud knock on the front door. "Mercy, now who can that be on a day like this?" she said. "Go see who it is, Joey."

While Joey ran to answer the door, Aunt Melinda

stepped over to the bookcase by the fireplace. She opened the glass doors and put the old leather-bound diary on the top shelf. Then she closed the doors and turned around expectantly as Joey ushered a well-dressed, middle-aged man into the parlor.

"Why James Larson," Aunt Melinda greeted him with a smile, "come in and have a cup of tea. What brings you out on such a stormy day?"

Without waiting for an answer, she turned to the twins. "This is my great-niece and great-nephew. Children, this is my friend, Mr. Larson, who manages the branch bank in the village across the lake."

Mr. Larson nodded to the twins and smiled when he saw the cheerful fire. "I would like nothing better than a visit, Melinda, but today I'm afraid I have come on business and cannot stay long."

Mr. Larson took a chair Aunt Melinda offered him and Jan and Joey gathered up the stack of empty dishes and took them to the kitchen.

"Boy, that guy would have to come to see Aunt Melinda just when she was going to tell us how to find the hidden tunnel," grumbled Joey in a low voice.

"Oh well, he said he couldn't stay long," his sister reminded him. "Let's surprise Aund Melinda and do the dishes."

Jan ran hot water into the sink and Joey walked across the kitchen to close the door to the parlor. Just as he was about to shut it, he overheard Aunt Melinda exclaim, "I don't know how I can find the money to pay off another mortgage, James."

Then he heard Mr. Larson reply, "Have you ever thought of selling White Meadow Farm, Melinda? Located right here on the lake, it would bring a good price."

"Joey!" Jan called from the sink.

Joey held his finger up to his lips and motioned for his sister to come over to the door. Jan wiped her hands on the dish towel and tiptoed across the kitchen.

"You shouldn't be eavesdropping on Aunt Melinda and Mr. Larson," she whispered with disapproval from behind the door.

"I know," Joey whispered back, "but this sounds funny to me, Jan. Just listen."

Aunt Melinda was talking now. Her voice was low, but they could make out what she was saying. "It would be hard for me to have to sell White Meadow Farm, James. It's been in the Howard family for four generations. It's the only home I know and I love it dearly."

Mr. Larson's deep, solemn voice replied, "Yes, I realize that, Melinda. Perhaps you can borrow the money somewhere. What about your nephew in Ohio? Couldn't he lend you the money?"

"Charles would be glad to help if he could," Aunt Melinda replied, "but I couldn't ask him. He has enough to do to keep his own small business going. Besides, he was more than generous in paying all the bills when Papa was sick for so long. I couldn't ask him for more."

Aunt Melinda paused and sighed regretfully. "If only I hadn't had all those extra repairs to make on the house last year."

49

"I know how hard it must be to keep up such a large place as this," Mr. Larson said with sympathy. "I wish I could help in some way, Melinda."

"You have done all that you can," replied Aunt Melinda, "and I appreciate that. Now I'll just have to pray and have faith that the Lord will see fit to let me live out my years in my own home. The Howards have always trusted in the Lord, James. He has provided for us in the past when troubles came. He will provide for me now, I am sure."

Mr. Larson reached over and patted Aunt Melinda's hand. "I wish I had your faith, Melinda."

"Nothing is impossible when you put your trust in the Lord, James," Aunt Melinda declared. Then she sat up straight and said, "Please don't say a word about this yet to anyone. I wouldn't want my great-niece and great-nephew to know about it. It would only spoil their vacation, and it might well be the last one they'll have at White Meadow Farm."

"I'll not breathe a word to anybody, Melinda. You know that," Mr. Larson promised. He leaned back in his chair. "Now, I believe I'll have that cup of tea after all."

Joey shut the door carefully without making a sound, and together he and Jan walked slowly back to the sink. For a long moment they were both quiet, then Jan spoke up. "Poor Aunt Melinda. Now we know why she wanted us to spend the rest of this summer at White Meadow Farm. It might be the last time we can be here."

"Yeah, and she didn't want us to know the reason why," Joey added. "I guess she doesn't want to worry anyone about her troubles."

"But we know about them now, and we've got to help her if we can."

"You know what she said, Jan. God will help her."

Jan nodded soberly. "That's right, Joey, but you know what Mom has often told us. We can't just sit back and let God do all the work. Sometimes He needs *our* help before He can help us."

Joey picked up the dish towel and polished the plate he was drying over and over while he thought about what his sister had just said. "Maybe there is a way we can help, Jan. Maybe we can find that chest of gold in the hidden tunnel. Finding that treasure would sure help Aunt Melinda pay off her mortgage."

Jan nodded doubtfully. "It sure would, but the Howards have been looking for that hidden treasure for generations and haven't found it."

Joey flung back his shoulders with determination. "Well, we'll find it because we *have* to."

Jan smiled at the stubborn tilt of her brother's head. "Then we'll try," she agreed. "Maybe the treasure has been waiting all these years for a time like this to be found."

When they finished the dishes, Aunt Melinda and Mr. Larson were still talking in the parlor.

"Won't he *ever* leave so that we can ask her about the hidden tunnel?" Joey grumbled. He was more anxious now than ever to start searching for the lost treasure.

"I guess he feels so bad about Aunt Melinda's money troubles that he decided to stay and visit with her after all," Jan reasoned.

51

Suddenly Joey got that faraway look in his eyes that came from his never being able to give up on an idea that bothered him. "I know what we can do. Let's hunt for the tunnel ourselves. Aunt Melinda said it was built from the barn to the house, so it must be somewhere under the stable. Let's start hunting for it there."

Jan glanced out the window. "It's still raining, but I guess it'll be all right."

They reached for their raincoats which were hung on wooden pegs along the kitchen wall. Inky ran to the door and begged to go with them. Joey opened the door and the cocker spaniel gamboled around them as they made their way across the porch.

The old barn looked dark and gloomy in the gray mist that rose up around it. Sagging on its weary timbers, it reminded Jan of a stooped old man huddled in the rain. It looked mysterious, too, she reflected, as if it had a secret to hide.

Patches raised her head and nickered a greeting when they opened the stable door. Jan walked over to the stall and talked to the pinto while Joey stood in the center of the stable and gazed around at the whitewashed walls and the stone floor.

"The tunnel would have to be underground." he reasoned, "so let's start searching the floor."

They shed their raincoats and started walking slowly back and forth, examining every inch of the smooth, flat stones in the stable floor in hopes of finding some kind of opening or trapdoor that might lead to the hidden tunnel.

Inky hunted, too, but not for a secret opening. He

hunted for bugs and mice and other crawling things, sniffing and growling into dark corners and the cracks between the stones.

They searched in the far corner behind a bale of straw and even in Patches' stall, but there was no sign of any passage entrance in the stable floor.

"Let's look in the tack room," Jan said at last, "Maybe the entrance to the hidden tunnel is in there somewhere".

With Inky trailing after them, they walked into the room in back of the stable. Old bridles and reins hung along the walls. They must have hung there for years, for they were cracked and coated with dust. In the middle of the room was a dusty old buckboard with large, iron-rimmed wheels and a high wooden seat.

"Will you look at that!" cried Joey and he couldn't resist scrambling up on the seat. "It's just like those old buggies they use in westerns on TV."

He reached for imaginary reins. "Giddy-up!" he called to a pair of imaginary horses. "Hang on!" he shouted to Jan, who had clambered up on the seat beside him. He jostled around on the seat, leaning over to give her shoulder a bump. "We have to make Cross Creek with the payroll by sundown."

"Whee!" squealed Jan. She turned around and looked behind her then leaned over to her brother and in a low voice whispered, "Joey, there are some outlaws following us. Hurry! Hurry!"

Joey clucked despairingly at the imaginary horses and gave the reins another shake. In a flash he remembered a hidden ravine behind the clump of trees up ahead. He urged the team on at full speed and reined them into the gully just in time to make their getaway.

"Whoa," he called, pulling hard on the reins.

Jan held her hand up to her ear. "They're riding past the gully, Yipee! We're safe!"

She caught her breath and they both laughed. It was fun playing make-believe on this old buckboard.

"I wonder how old this thing is," Jan said.

"Ancient," Joey replied, jumping down from the high seat. "I'll bet our great-great-great-grandfather used it. We can have lots of fun playing on it, but now we'd better hunt for that hidden tunnel."

They searched the stone floor underneath the dusty harnesses. "There's nothing here but cobwebs," Jan grumbled with disgust as she pulled a big sticky web out of her hair.

On hands and knees they searched the stones underneath the buckboard but found no trapdoor nor opening of any kind there either.

Let's hunt back in the stable again," Joey suggested. He flung his head back with more determination that ever. "An opening to that tunnel has got to be *somewhere.*"

"*Hidden* tunnel sure is a good name for it," declared Jan.

But a second search of the stable floor revealed nothing further. Inky got tired of following them around and curled up in the straw in Patches' stall. The pinto chewed her oats contentedly and gazed at them with large, wondering eyes.

Wearily Joey threw himself down on the bale of straw in the corner. Resting his chin in the palms of his hands, he said, "Now *where* could the entrance to that tunnel be?"

His blue eyes rolled upward in thought and suddenly he jumped up and pointed to the ceiling over his head. "Hey, I found a trapdoor! Look up there!"

"A trapdoor in the ceiling isn't going to lead to an underground tunnel," Jan told him.

"I know but I'm going to climb up there anyway," Joey declared. "While we're at it, we might as well explore the entire barn."

Jan shook her head. She sometimes wondered about her brother's logic.

Joey scrambled up a ladder that was built into the wall and pushed open the little door in the ceiling. He lifted himself through the opening and onto the big barn floor. He discovered that there was another wall ladder right next to the trapdoor that led up into the hayloft.

"Come on up," he called down to his sister.

Reluctantly Jan followed her brother's voice. But she didn't climb the wall ladder through the trapdoor. Instead she used the steps that led up into the main part of the barn.

"It's awfully dark up here," she said as she stepped out onto the big barn floor. "And spooky too."

Joey walked over to the double doors in front of the barn and pushed them apart. They creaked loudly on their ancient metal rollers but opened wide enough to send a shaft of light across the floor. "There, that's better," he said. "Now we can see."

Jan still had a creepy feeling as she looked up at

the dark beams, festooned with dusty cobwebs, and at the lofts that flanked both sides of the barn like huge shelves. Underneath the lofts were dark, mysterious shadows. She ventured a step forward, but when a sudden, low, wavering noise sounded above her, she quickly grabbed her brother's arm.

"What--what was that?"

Next there came a fluttering sound, high up in the lofts. Through the shaft of light from the open doors, dark wings swooped down and lighted on the beam right above their heads.

"It's only pigeons," Joey told her. "They must have come into the barn to get out of the rain. See them sitting up there?"

"I see them now," Jan said with relief as she peered up at the round gray forms perched on the barn rafters.

They listened to the low cooing for a while longer. Then Jan poked her head underneath one of the dark lofts. She gave a quick cry and stepped back suddenly.

"Now what's the matter?" asked Joey.

"Yuk! Something damp and sticky just brushed against my face. It felt like a bat's wing."

Joey, who wasn't afraid of bats, walked bravely underneath the loft and came out brushing off the sticky remains of a big cobweb.

"You must have burst in on a spider's mansion," he said, grinning. "I never saw such a big web."

He looked up at the lofts. "I'm going to explore the haymow."

As agile as a monkey, he scampered up the loft ladder. Up he climbed until he was balancing himself on the side beam that ran along the top of the mow.

"Oh boy!" he shouted. "It's neat up here and there's still some hay left in the loft." Grinning down at his sister, he said, "watch this!" And taking a running jump from the beam, he went sailing through the air and into the haymow below.

"Wow, this is great!" he cried, jumping up and down in the hay. "Come on up."

It did look like fun, so Jan scampered up the ladder and was soon balancing herself on the wide beam with her brother.

"Let's join hands and jump into the hay together," she said.

"All right," Joey agreed. Taking hands, they shut their eyes tightly and squealed with delight as they sailed through the air, landing in the soft hay below. Up they bounced with hay in their hair and bits of scratchy hay down their backs, but what fun it was jumping in the big mow!

"This is as much fun as jumping off a diving board at a pool," Jan said.

"I'll go along with that!" shouted Joey, leaping up and down in the springy hay like a jumping jack. "We can have lots of fun playing in this old barn." He bounced over to where his sister was standing and put his hand on her shoulder. "You're *it* for tag!"

"Oh no I'm not!" Jan snapped, but before she had a chance to reach out to tag him back, Joey was scrambling to the top of the loft again.

"I'll catch you yet," Jan warned as she climbed up after him.

57

But Joey was too swift for his sister. Nimbly he walked across the beam high above the barn floor. "Can't catch me!" he called, daring her to follow him across the beam to the loft on the other side.

Joey teased his sister by sitting down on the high beam and grinning across at her. "Can't catch me!" he kept chanting.

Jan was about to climb up after him when, just at that moment, she heard something that made her stop and listen. It was a loud rustling sound that seemed to be coming from the haymow across the way.

Joey heard it, too, and started to edge his way back across the high beam. When he reached the other side where Jan stood, he whispered, "Something's moving around in the hayloft over there."

Jan nodded. "I know. I heard it too. Maybe it's some kind of animal."

But before Joey had a chance to reply, there came another sound, this time from somewhere underneath the dark loft. It sounded like stealthy footsteps creeping away!

Nimbly Joey walked across the beam high above the barn floor. "Can't catch me!" he called, daring Jan to follow him.

5

A GHOSTLY LIGHT AND
WATCHING EYES

"THAT WAS no animal!" Joey exclaimed in a half whisper. "Did you hear those footsteps?"

Jan nodded, her eyes round with fright. "But I don't hear them now."

Before they could say another word, a shrill bark sounded underneath the barn, followed by a loud whinny and a stamping of hoofs on the stable floor.

"Somebody's in the stable," Jan gasped. "Listen to Inky and Patches!"

Joey scrambled down the loft ladder as fast as he

could manage and Jan scooted down right behind him. They landed on the barn floor about the same time. Picking themselves up, they dashed down the steps that led into the stable. They stood motionless for a moment, looking bewilderedly around them.

"Where did he go?" Joey said. In the same breath he directed, "Look in the tack room, Jan, and I'll take a look outside."

Without another word, they headed in opposite directions. Inky didn't follow Joey outside. He was too busy fussing around in the far corner of the stable.

Minutes later when Joey returned, he reported breathlessly, "I ran all around the barn and out as far as the road. I looked over the meadow, too, and didn't see anybody."

"I couldn't find anybody here, either." Jan looked around her with questioning eyes. "Where could he have disappeared to so quickly?"

She reached up to rub Patches on the nose. "I wish you could talk, girl, then you could tell us who was here." But the pinto only shook her head and fluttered her nostrils at them.

Inky was still fussing around in the far corner of the stable. He was growling and sniffing curiously around the bale of straw.

"What's the matter with him?" Joey asked as he walked over to see what was bothering the dog. He glanced down at the bale. It was the same bale of straw he had sat on when he had discovered the trapdoor in the ceiling. But now there was something different about it. His brow furrowed in perplexity. Finally he figured out what it was.

"Hey, this bale has been moved!" he cried. "It was farther back in the corner." Then his eye caught something that made him shout, "Jan, look!"

There in the floor of the stable where the bale of straw had been before was what looked like a wooden door with a large iron ring fastened to it.

Peering over her brother's shoulder, Jan breathed, "A trapdoor! We didn't notice it before."

"That's because this bale of straw was placed over it and hid it from view," Joey said. "That is, before it was moved."

"Do you think it leads down to the hidden tunnel?"

"I'd bet my bottom dollar on it." Joey reached over to grasp the ring. "Let's see."

He was about to pull open the trapdoor when the sound of a dinner bell rang out from the direction of the house.

"That must be Aunt Melinda's bell," Jan said. "I'll bet she wants us."

"Aw shoot," grumbled Joey, "I don't want to leave now--just when we have probably found the entrance to the hidden tunnel."

Jan reached for their raincoats. "We better see what she wants. We can come back later."

Joey looked longingly at the trapdoor. But Aunt Melinda's bell kept ringing loudly and persistently. Maybe she would be angry if they didn't come at once. Reluctantly he followed his sister out of the stable. As they crossed the yard, they noticed that Mr. Larson's car was no longer parked in the lane.

When Joey caught up with Jan, he warned, "Let's

62

not tell Aunt Melinda about those footsteps we heard in the barn. It might worry her to think there was a prowler there and she might not let us play in the barn any more."

Jan nodded agreement and led the way up the back porch steps.

Aunt Melinda was waiting for them in the kitchen. "I was wondering where you got to," she said. "That's why I rang this old dinner bell. Any time you hear it, you'll know I want you. It saves calling."

Although Aunt Melinda sounded cheerful enough, she couldn't hide those little worry lines around her eyes. *She's thinking about that mortgage money*, Jan thought. And to get her great-aunt's mind off her troubles, she said, "Guess what, Aunt Melinda, we found a trapdoor in the floor of the stable. Does it lead to the hidden tunnel?"

Aunt Melinda's face brightened. "Yes, it does. It's hidden under a bale of straw. That was good hunting."

"We haven't explored the tunnel yet," Joey told her. "Could we explore it now?"

Aunt Melinda shook her head. "Not today. It's too damp to go outside again."

"It's stopped raining," Joey begged.

But Aunt Melinda was firm. "Just the same, you'd better play in the house."

The twins sighed. Aunt Melinda was beginning to sound just like Mom.

At the look of disappointment on their faces, Aunt Melinda suggested, "While we still have some

63

fire left, what do you say we pop some corn? I'll get the popcorn and you two can get the popper in the pantry."

The twins went for the corn popper and before long they were in the parlor, seated on the floor in front of the fireplace. Soon the tempting aroma of hot, buttered popcorn filled the old farmhouse, and for the rest of the afternoon they ate popcorn and played Scrabble.

That night another shower came up and they all went to bed early. Jan couldn't go to sleep right away. She lay awake a long time, listening to the steady downpour of rain and the sound of the wind moaning in the eaves of the old house. From the downstairs landing the grandfather clock chimed ten deep tones.

Jan blinked in the darkness and thought about all the things that had happened their first day at White Meadow Farm. She thought about Aunt Melinda's surprise in the barn and how much fun it had been riding Patches. She thought about finding the secret room in the attic and Martha Howard's diary which told about the secret tunnel and about the chest of gold that was hidden there.

Will we ever find the lost treasure so that Aunt Melinda can pay off her mortgage and keep the farm? Jan wondered. *It's strange how terribly important that is to me now, when just a few days ago Joey and I couldn't have cared less about what happened to White Meadow Farm.*

Jan moved about restlessly in bed as she remembered with a little chill of uneasiness, the footsteps they had heard in the barn while they were playing in the hayloft and how mysteriously the prowler had disappeared. Why would someone be prowling around inside Aunt Melinda's barn, not wanting to be seen?

Suddenly she heard footsteps again. Only this time they were outside her bedroom door! Jan sat straight up in bed. The door opened slowly and Joey poked his head in. "Are you awake?"

"Uh huh. Come in."

Joey made his way across the room and stood by her bed. "I can't get to sleep, either," he told her. "I keep wondering about those footsteps we heard in the barn and who besides ourselves would be there on a rainy afternoon and why would he want to sneak away like that?"

"I've been wondering the same thing, too," Jan said. "Do you think whoever it was moved that bale of straw and hid in the tunnel when he heard us coming?"

Joey was quiet for a minute. Then he exclaimed softly, "Of course! Why didn't we think of that sooner? That must have been how he got away so fast."

"And if he knows about the hidden tunnel, he might know about the treasure, too," Jan added in alarm.

"Then we'd better get busy searching for that chest of gold," Joey said. "Let's start looking for it first thing in the morning."

A sudden gust of wind blew some rain against the open window and splattered it on the sill. Jan slipped away from her bed to close the window. She stood a moment to peer out into the dark, wet night. She was about to turn away and hop back into bed when a flicker of lightning brightened the sky. The outlines of the old barn flashed momentarily into view.

Jan blinked her eyes, but all was darkness again—or was it? The next moment she caught her breath and gasped, "Joey! Come here!"

With a thump in the dark Joey bounded across the room in one convulsive leap. "What's the matter?" he whispered nervously.

"Look—down in the meadow!"

Joey peered through the wet blackness. Then he saw the dim light, too, moving across the dark meadow in the direction of the barn. It was a thin, yellow glow, moving in jerky motions as if someone in a great hurry was running with it.

The twins crouched down beside the window, paralyzed with fear as they watched the wavering light. It was raining so hard now and the night was so dark that they couldn't see who it was carrying the light. The yellow beam just seemed to be floating in quick jerky motions across the dark meadow.

At last Jan found her voice. In little more than a whisper, she said, "It—it's a stormy night, Joey, and there's a light in the meadow coming toward the barn. Could it—could it be the ghost Martha Howard wrote about in her diary?"

Joey was too startled to argue with her about ghosts. He just crouched closer to the window and watched the pale ghost-light until it disappeared into the barn.

For several long moments they lingered by the

window, staring out into the stormy night. When he found his voice, Joey said, "Maybe it's the prowler we heard in the barn today."

"But why would he want to come back to the barn tonight—in the storm?" Jan wondered.

"Maybe he's some old tramp and he came back to the barn to get out of the rain."

In hushed voices they exclaimed over and over about what they had just seen and how strange it was for anyone to be out in the meadow on such a stormy night. They waited for the light to reappear, but the meadow remained dark. There was no light in the barn, either, where it had disappeared.

Finally Joey said, "I guess we better get back to bed. If we're going to search that tunnel tomorrow, we've got to be wide-awake."

He started for his own room and Jan called after him in a loud whisper, "Let's leave our doors open. That way we won't be so alone in our rooms."

Joey was willing enough. "Good night," he mumbled as he made his way across the hall. It was comforting to hear his footfalls on the squeaky old boards of his room and the bed creak in the darkness as he got into it.

Even though Jan thought she'd never be able to get a wink of sleep for the rest of that stormy night, her eyelids did grow heavy and before the grandfather clock at the bottom of the stairway struck eleven deep tones, she had drifted off to sleep.

The bright morning sun, slanting through the window and across Jan's bed, awakened her the next morning. She leaped out of bed and ran to the window. After the rain, the new-washed meadow was fresh and bright. Below it the waters of the lake sparkled blue and silver in the sunshine. The old barn was so peaceful-looking in the morning brightness that what they had seen there the night before seemed to Jan like a bad dream.

Remembering what they had planned to do that day, she got dressed as fast as she could and hurried down the stairs. Joey had been the first one up that morning, and through the kitchen door she could see him seated at the table.

"My, I'm glad that storm is over," Aunt Melinda said as Jan sat down across from her brother. "I hope it didn't keep you two awake last night."

Joey threw a warning glance at his sister and Jan read his thoughts. Aunt Melinda had enough to worry about without telling her about the mysterious light in the meadow. Besides, she didn't believe in the ghost and might think that, like Martha Howard, they had just imagined it.

The twins started eating without saying a word. Aunt Melinda poured herself a cup of coffee and sat at the table with them. "It's a bright, blue day," she said with expectancy. "There'll be a lot of summer people out on the lake today."

"Are there many cottages around the lake?" asked Jan. "I haven't seen any."

"You can't see them in the summer," Aunt Melinda told her. "They are all tucked back behind the trees. But in the winter when the leaves are off the trees, you can see them. There aren't many on this side of the lake, but there are quite a few on the other side where the village is."

As soon as they had finished their bacon and eggs, Aunt Melinda had a favor to ask. "I'll do the dishes this morning if you two will pick me some blueberries in the meadow—enough for two pies."

Joey rolled his blue eyes at Jan and there was dismay in their look.

"What's the matter with you two?" Aunt Melinda asked, "don't you like blueberry pie?"

"Oh-oh, yes," Jan replied. "It's just that we had planned to search for the lost treasure today."

"That's right," Joey added. "We wanted to get an early start."

"It won't take all day to pick berries," Aunt Melinda told them. "Pick the largest and the darkest ones. The lighter ones aren't quite ripe yet."

She went into the pantry and returned with two berry pails. Inky bounced out of the kitchen ahead of them and led the way to the meadow, his long silky ears flapping out like sails as he ran.

"You might know when we wanted to search for the hidden tunnel, Aunt Melinda would be in the mood for making blueberry pies," Joey grumbled as he glanced wistfully at the old barn.

Jan drew in deep breaths of fresh morning air. "If we hurry, we'll still have lots of time. Anyway, it's nice being in the meadow this time of day."

Inky ran ahead to join Patches, who was grazing at the far side of the meadow.

"Aunt Melinda must have let Patches out early," Jan said. Then she laughed. "Look, you can hardly see Inky."

The meadow was so lush that all they could see of the little black dog was a zigzag path of waving green grass. Locusts hummed in the nearby trees and in the tall weeds grasshoppers popped up at them in all directions. All around them bloomed hundreds of white, lacy flowers. The entire meadow was white with them, just as Dad had remembered it.

Jan bent over to pick one of the Queen Anne's lace. "See, Joey, it does look like lace," she pointed out as she examined the wild flower closely, "and it's pretty enough to be a queen's."

They waded through the tall grass and wild flowers until they found the blueberry bushes.

"Oh boy," Joey cried when he saw all the dark ripe berries. "It shouldn't take us long to pick enough for two pies. Let's have a race and see who can fill a pail first."

He began picking at once. Jan could hear the ring of the berries as they dropped into the bottom of his empty pail. Joey might have a head start, but Jan decided to search for the bushes where the largest berries grew. She followed the blueberry patch to the far side of the meadow where the grove of pines rose up from the lake. She was soon rewarded in her search, for there she found bushes that hung heavy with the largest blueberries she had ever seen.

"You have to hunt for the big ones," she called back to her brother as she started to fill her pail. She giggled as she picked. She knew that Joey would eat as many berries as he picked, so it shouldn't be too hard to beat him.

Jan had her pail half filled when Patches came wandering over to her. The curious little horse nickered and nuzzled the pockets of her jeans.

Jan laughed. "I'll bet the McNeils keep raw carrots or lumps of sugar in their pockets for you."

She held out the palm of her hand with a berry on it. Patches wrinkled up her soft velvety nose at the berry and walked away. Berries weren't carrots or sugar!

Jan continued picking and soon her pail was full. She was about to call back to Joey that she was the first one finished when she heard him cry out, "Watch it, Patches!" The next moment he gave an agonizing groan.

Jan left her pail and hurried over to where her brother had been picking. "What's the matter?" she called. She stopped short and stared down at the overturned pail and the mound of berries scattered over the ground.

"Now look what you've done, clumsy," Joey shouted crossly at Patches. "And I had my pail almost full!"

Jan reached up to smooth the pinto's ruffled mane. "You didn't mean to kick over Joey's pail, did you, girl?"

Patches lowered her head and nickered. Then she turned and nudged the boy playfully on the back of the neck.

Joey couldn't stay angry long. His round freckled face wrinkled up in a grin. "Okay, Patches," he said, "I guess I'll just have to watch my pail with you around."

"I'll help pick up the berries," Jan offered. "We can get most of them back in the pail."

"Are you finished picking?"

"Oh, long ago," Jan exaggerated.

Joey groaned and began to pick the spilled berries off the ground. When most of them were back in the pail, Jan said, "Come over where I was picking. The berries are bigger and it won't take so long to fill your pail—if you don't eat so many!"

Joey followed her to the far side of the meadow. When he saw how big the berries were, he started to pick at once.

Jan looked around for her pail. She was searching for it in the tall grass where she thought she left it, when she heard something rustle—louder than a bird—in the pine woods nearby. She stopped to listen. The next moment there was a loud snap, as if a foot had come down on a fallen tree branch.

Jan looked up suddenly. Was there a shadow moving between those dark trees? As she stood staring at the pines, she had the queer feeling that somebody was watching them.

"Joey!" she whispered back over her shoulder. "I think there's somebody in the pines over there."

Joey looked up with startled eyes. But the dark trees stood silent and empty again.

"You must have been imagining it," he said. "Hurry up and help me fill my pail."

"But I heard a branch snap over there," Jan insisted, "and I thought I saw something move between those trees."

"Probably just a squirrel or a rabbit," Joey told her.

Jan found her pail, but as she was returning to the bushes where Joey was picking, she felt more than ever that watching eyes were following her.

6

EXPLORING THE TUNNEL

AUNT MELINDA was so pleased with the berries they had brought her that she told them they could do whatever they wished for the rest of the day.

Joey ran up to his room for his flashlight. When he came bouncing downstairs again, they started for the barn. Coming in from the bright sunlight, they found the stable dim and shadowy. It seemed lonesome and empty without Patches.

Remembering the creepy footsteps they had

heard yesterday and the ghostly light they had seen entering the barn in the storm last night, Jan peered anxiously around her. She kept glancing over her shoulder into the dark corners as if she half expected to see the ghost of Amos Brown reappear inside the stable.

Joey made his way to the far corner. He stopped suddenly and stared. "Hey, the bale of straw is back over the trapdoor again. Look, it's just as it was yesterday when we first came to the stable."

Jan hurried to his side. "The prowler we heard in the barn yesterday must have put it back," she said. "Probably he didn't want us to find the trapdoor."

"Yeah, it looks that way," agreed Joey, bending over the bale. "Give me a hand. Help me move it."

Together they pushed the heavy bale of straw to one side. The next minute they were on their hands and knees, bending over the big iron ring in the middle of the wooden plank. Joey reached over and pulled up on the ring. Slowly the trapdoor opened and Jan's heart did a flip-flop as she peered down into the square black hole in the stable floor.

"Look, there are steps leading down," Joey said, pointing to a row of narrow stone steps disappearing into the darkness below.

He leaped to his feet and started down the steps. Inky, who had followed them into the barn, growled as he watched Joey's head disappear through the dark opening.

When Joey reached the bottom step, Jan called down, "Are you in the tunnel? What's it like down there?"

"Join me and find out," came her brother's muffled voice in reply.

Slowly Jan descended the narrow, stone steps. At the bottom she blinked at the dark passageway. Joey's light could not penetrate very far and a long, black emptiness stretched out before them.

"It-it's spooky down here," Jan said in a quavering voice.

"Come on, let's start exploring," Joey urged.

Jan hesitated. "Suppose something's down here? Suppose something or somebody's waiting for us up ahead in the darkness?"

Joey rolled his eyes teasingly in her direction. "You mean like the ghost?"

A shiver crept down Jan's spine, but she didn't want her brother to think that she still half-believed in the ghost so she answered, "I mean it could be that prowler."

"Nobody's here now or that bale of straw wouldn't be over the trapdoor," Joey told her. "Come on."

The tunnel became pitch black after they had taken a few steps away from the open trapdoor. Inky remained on the top step, whimpering softly for them. Jan called to him, but he just stayed there and wouldn't come down.

"I guess he doesn't like dark tunnels," she said. "I read somewhere that a dog will never go where there's a ghost."

"Oh, come on!" Joey started forward again, but Jan thought she detected a tone of uncertainty in his own voice.

He flashed his light around the tunnel and its

75

beam wavered over the brick walls and low passageway. Here and there a trickle of water dripped down from heavy wooden beams that shored up the sides of the tunnel and supported the roof. It was cool and damp and the air was musty and close. It reminded Jan of an underground cave she and Joey had once been in.

Joey moved slowly along the shadowy brick walls and Jan followed closely behind him. Now and then he threw the beam along the narrow walls and up to the roof to see if there might be a place where the treasure could be hidden. Jan felt along the damp bricks with her hands to see if any of them were loose and might come out, revealing a secret hiding place.

But the walls seemed solid enough and the bricks were lined evenly. Joey turned the flashlight on the earthen floor of the tunnel. It was damp and slippery with smoothly packed ground that had been trod over by a countless number of feet through the years.

"Just think, Joey, real runaway slaves used to pass through here. It must have been exciting and a little scary for them in those days." Jan could imagine the fright and anxiety of a runaway making his way through this long, dark tunnel.

They moved on. The passage continued in a straight line, but they couldn't tell in what direction it was going.

Joey's light could not penetrate very far. A long, black emptiness stretched out before them. "It-it's spooky down here," Jan said in a quavering voice.

After a while Joey said, "Aunt Melinda told us the tunnel comes out in the house, but I wonder where."

"I hope we find out soon," Jan whispered. "I didn't think it would be so long."

"It probably isn't that long," Joey told her. "It just seems that way because it's so dark and narrow and we have to go so slow."

All of a sudden the tunnel took a sharp turn to the left. Jan's skin prickled. "I wonder what's beyond that turn?"

"I'll find out," Joey said quickly, slipping around the turn and leaving her alone in the dark.

A moment later there was a scary, wailing sound in the darkness ahead. At first Jan's heart thumped in terror, then she became angry when she realized that it was only Joey, trying to scare her.

"Oh, stop it," she said crossly. "You'd be scared silly, too, if you met somebody—or something in here. You'd better cut out horsing around and keep looking for the treasure. That's what we came here for."

Joey stopped his wailing and started to giggle as Jan moved quickly around the turn. They continued on, examining carefully the brick walls and dirt floor.

"So far it doesn't look as if the treasure's anywhere in this tunnel," Joey said.

"It's as clean as a whistle," Jan added with a sigh, using their father's favorite expression. "There's not even a brick or board or a nail out of place."

Now the dark passage seemed to slope upward. *It must be coming to an end,* Jan thought, *but where?*

They crept along until Joey's light fell on a solid wooden wall that blocked their way. "Oh, wow!" he said, stopping dead still.

He played his beam over the wall. There was no way around it that he could see. Had they come to a dead end? Had the tunnel been boarded up here for some reason?

"It can't end here!" Joey exclaimed in a puzzled tone of voice. "It has to come out somewhere in the house."

"Maybe this wall isn't as solid as it looks," Jan suggested, remembering the false wall of the secret room in the attic.

Together they leaned against the boards and pushed. To their surprise the wall swung inward with a groaning sound and they found themselves in a small room lined with shelves. Joey swept his light over the shelves and they discovered that they were filled with jars of canned fruit and vegetables. Against the opposite wall of the room was a large screened-in wooden frame in which two freshly baked blueberry pies were cooling

Jan glanced about her, filled with curiosity. "We must be in Aunt Melinda's fruit cellar."

Joey let the wall to the tunnel swing shut. On back of it was more shelving. As it closed, it fit into place with the other shelves so that you couldn't tell that there was an entrance to the tunnel there at all.

The twins walked over to a door that led to the main part of the cellar. Light from the kitchen above drew them like a magnet up the cellar steps.

"Aunt Melinda!" they called as they clumped up

79

the stairs. They were eager to tell her that they had explored the entire tunnel and had found where it had come out in the fruit cellar.

But when they entered the kitchen, it was empty. Jan noticed that the sink was filled with unwashed baking dishes, but Aunt Melinda was nowhere around. The twins looked at one another questioningly. It wasn't like their great-aunt to leave the kitchen in such an untidy state.

"Listen," Jan said, "I think I hear her talking to someone in front of the house."

They followed the sound of voices through the parlor to the front door where Aunt Melinda was saying goodbye to a caller.

He was an ordinary-looking man of average height, with pale brown hair receding from a high forehead. It was his sharp, penetrating, gray eyes and the way his calloused fingers twisted nervously around a ring of car keys as he stepped out on the front porch that made him appear a bit unusual.

He threw a quick glance at the twins, then with a brief nod to Aunt Melinda, he hurried over to his blue Ford and drove off.

"Who was that?" Joey asked.

But their great-aunt just shook her head and said, "What a time to have a caller, right in the middle of cleaning up my baking dishes."

She hustled back to the kitchen and the twins hurried after her.

"Guess what! We found the hidden tunnel," Jan informed her, "and we followed it all the way from the stable to the fruit cellar."

"But we didn't find the treasure," Joey added, his

voice low with disappointment.

Aunt Melinda smiled. "Well, you searched for it only this one time. Maybe another time you'll have better luck. Now I have news. That man who was just here wants to rent a room for a week. I told him about the motel across the lake but he said he'd rather stay here where it's quiet,"

"Are you going to let him stay?" asked Jan.

"Well, I never thought about taking in summer boarders before," Aunt Melinda replied, "but if he'd rather be here than at the motel, I'll let him stay. We have more than enough bedrooms in this old house, and what he offered to pay for one will certainly come in handy."

Aunt Melinda put on her apron and started washing the baking dishes. "Would you two run upstairs to that big front bedroom and pull up all the windows and open the blinds?" she asked. "That room has been closed for so long that I'd like to air it out and get it ready. Mr. Grimes will be here for supper."

"Is that his name?" asked Joey.

Aunt Melinda nodded and started running water into the sink. The twins hurried up the stairs to the big bedroom in front of the house. As they pushed up windows and opened shutters, they talked about the new boarder.

"Aunt Melinda seems real happy to be renting him this room," Jan said.

"Well, Mr. Grimes offered to pay her good money for it," Joey replied, "and that's what she needs right now more than anything else."

Jan flopped down on the big four-poster bed and

watched the lace curtains flap in the breeze at the open windows.

"I wonder why Aunt Melinda never thought about taking in boarders before. With this big house she could make lots of money."

Joey opened the door to the wardrobe and stuck his head inside. "I guess she thought that most people would want to stay at the motel."

"But Mr. Grimes didn't," Jan replied.

"Well, maybe he's the quiet type and that's why he didn't want to stay there—too many people."

"He seemed awfully nervous about something," Jan said, remembering how his fingers had twisted around the ring of car keys.

"That's all the more reason why he'd want to be away from people," Joey reasoned.

"But don't you think it's funny that he asked Aunt Melinda to rent a room here at White Meadow Farm when there isn't even a tourist sign or anything outside?" Jan persisted. "Why would he stop right here at this particular house and ask for a room?"

Joey jerked his head out of the wardrobe. "I never thought about that. Oh well, maybe someone in the village told him about White Meadow Farm, and maybe he's partial to old farmhouses." He looked at his sister and grinned. "Come on, Miss Worry Wart, let's go down and ask Aunt Melinda when lunch is going to be ready. I'm starved."

7

THE MISSING PIE

AFTER LUNCH the twins decided to search the hidden tunnel again. Now that they knew its route and where it came out, they could spend more time in earnest hunting for the lost treasure. But first Jan thought they should exercise Patches, so they each took a turn riding her.

When it was Jan's turn, she guided the pinto up the lane. The little horse pricked her ears, her head held high, and her tail arched proudly. When they reached the road, Jan squeezed Patches' sides with her legs and the pinto trotted off at a brisk pace.

Up and down the road they cantered several times, then Jan reined in Patches to a walk and gave her her head to see where she would go. The pinto started back toward the meadow. She made her way through the Queen Anne's lace until she came to a patch of green grass near the grove of pines.

While the little horse grazed, Jan stared idly at the pine woods. A frisky squirrel ran up the trunk of one of the trees and chattered noisily. Red-crested woodpeckers darted in and out between the pine boughs. Jan remembered the moving shadow she had seen through these dark trees that morning. *I was foolish to have been frightened,* she told herself. *These woods must be filled with all kinds of birds and animals.*

She was about to turn Patches back to the stable when a sudden loud snap sounded from the pines. Jan's eyes flew back to the dark trees. Patches pricked up her ears and fluttered her nostrils. Before Jan could stop her, the pinto bolted toward the woods.

Another branch cracked loudly in the pines, then Jan saw the moving shadow again. But this time it took no precautions to be stealthy. Jan reined in Patches, just as a slim figure emerged from behind a tree.

With wide eyes Jan stared at a girl about her own age with long brown hair falling over her shoulders. The girl's hazel eyes were laughing as she held out the palm of her hand with a lump of sugar on it.

Patches didn't need a second invitation. She

walked over to the girl and with her soft velvety nose took the sugar right out of her hand. By the way the girl reached up and stroked Patches' long nose, Jan could tell that she knew a lot about horses. As she watched this strange girl, a sudden thought came to her.

"This is your horse, isn't it?"

The girl smiled. "I'm Heather McNeil. You must be Miss Melinda's great-niece. She told us you and your brother were coming."

"Were you in the pinewoods this morning when we were picking berries?" Jan asked curiously.

Heather nodded. "At first I wasn't sure who you were, so I watched you from the woods. I couldn't stay to meet you. We had just arrived, and Mom said I could come over and take just one quick look at Patches before helping her unpack."

Jan dismounted and handed the reins to Heather. "Here's your horse. She sure is great."

"Oh, finish your ride," Heather said. "I'm glad Patches has someone to exercise her when we're not here."

"Could we both ride her?"

"Sure," Heather replied. "You get back in the saddle and give me a hand up. I'll ride behind you."

Together the two girls rode Patches back to the barn. Joey was sitting on the barnyard fence watching them.

"Heather, this is my brother, Joey," Jan said when they dismounted.

Heather walked up to the fence. "Hi, Joey."

"Hi," Joey replied in the offhand manner he always used when meeting a strange girl.

Heather glanced from Joey to Jan. "You look enough alike to be twins," she commented.

"We are," Jan told her.

"I bet it's fun having a twin," Heather said.

Jan grinned over at Joey. "Oh, it has its good points—sometimes."

"And its bad ones," Joey teased back.

"I don't have any brothers or sisters." Heather said wistfully. "And there are no kids my age anywhere near our cottage. There are no older kids to play with unless I go down to the motel, but Daddy doesn't want me to use their dock to swim from when we have a dock of our own."

"How did you get way over here?" asked Joey.

"I rowed over in our boat." Heather pointed to Aunt Melinda's dock that stretched out over the lake. Alongside an old wooden rowboat was a shining aluminum one. Jan guessed the aluminum one belonged to the McNeils.

"Do you want to ride Patches now?" Heather asked, holding the rein out to Joey.

"No, thanks. I had a ride before Jan had hers." Joey slid down from the fence and walked toward the stable. "I'm going to take another look at that hidden tunnel."

As soon as he said those words, he stopped short. He wished he hadn't spoken about the hidden tunnel in front of Heather, a stranger. But the words had just slipped out. He swung around and looked at the strange girl, not knowing what to say next.

"Joey," Jan spoke up, "maybe Heather could help us hunt for the lost treasure."

Joey groaned inwardly as his sister let out

86

another secret. He kept watching Heather, who hadn't missed a word.

"A hidden tunnel? A lost treasure?" She was wide-eyed with wonder.

"Please, Joey," Jan pleaded. "Heather has nobody to play with and she's willing to share Patches with us. Maybe she can help us find the treasure."

Joey glanced from the friendly new girl to his sister. "Well, okay," he said reluctantly, "but she has to promise not to tell a soul if we let her in on it."

"You have my solemn word," Heather said and her voice was as serious as the look on her face.

"Don't even tell your parents," Joey cautioned. "If word gets out that there is a lost treasure in the tunnel, this whole place will be swarming with treasure-seekers."

"I *promise, promise, promise* not to tell," Heather vowed. "Now what about the hidden tunnel and the lost treasure?"

Taking turns, the twins told their friend about finding Martha Howard's diary in the attic and about Aunt Melinda's account of the treasure that was never found. Jan ended by telling about the creepy footsteps in the loft and the strange light they had seen in the meadow last night.

Heather wrapped her arms around her and whispered with delight, "Wow, it sure sounds spooky!" Then she added, "I'd love to help you hunt for that treasure. We're going to stay at White Meadow Lake for two whole weeks this time because Daddy has his vacation. Maybe we can find the treasure while I'm here. I hope so."

"So do we," Jan said.

87

"Then let's get right at it." Joey picked up a hammer he had found in the toolshed and led the way into the stable. The bale of straw was to one side where they had moved it that morning. Jan helped him open the trapdoor and soon three heads were peering through the dark square in the stable floor.

"I'll go first," Joey said. "You can hand me down that hammer."

"What's it for?" Jan wanted to know.

"You'll see," Joey told her as he edged his way through the trapdoor. "There, I'm down the steps now," he called up to the girls. "Come on down."

He snapped on his flashlight so they could see. Jan handed him the hammer then started through the trapdoor. Heather followed.

"It sure is dark down here," Heather said. Her voice sounded hollow as it echoed through the long passageway.

While Jan held the flashlight, Joey started tapping the brick walls with the hammer. "Now listen and tell me if these bricks sound different when I tap them," he instructed the girls. "If they sound hollow, there might be a hiding place behind them where the treasure is hidden."

Jan trained the light on the hammer and they listened carefully as Joey tapped on the bricks. But each brick sounded the same as the others. Joey kept tapping until they were halfway through the tunnel. Then he stopped and leaned wearily against the wall. "No luck so far," he said.

"You know what," Jan said thoughtfully. "We may be hunting for the treasure at the wrong end of the tunnel."

"What do you mean by that?"

"I mean that John Howard might have hidden the chest of gold at the other end, close to the house where it would be safer."

"I never thought of that," Joey admitted. "I'll bet that's just what he did do. Come on, let's search the other end by the fruit cellar."

With Jan leading the way with the flashlight, they hurried through the dark passage. When they came to the far end, Joey started tapping the walls again. They were sure they would find the mysterious hiding place now. But when they made their way toward the center of the tunnel again and still had no luck, they became more discouraged than ever.

"No hollow places behind these bricks," moaned Joey.

"Maybe the treasure was found a long time ago," Heather suggested, "and nobody knew about it."

But the twins shook their heads. "Our ancestors have been hunting for it for years," Joey explained. "If it had been found, somebody in the family would have told the others about it." He added in a low, discouraged tone of voice, "I wonder if it'll ever be found."

They fell silent. Jan looked about her at the empty passage. Where in this long, dark tunnel could the lost treasure be?

"Oh, well," she said with determined cheerfulness, "you know what Aunt Melinda said. Nothing is impossible when you put your trust in the Lord. Maybe the treasure isn't hidden in the walls but somewhere else in the tunnel. We'll find it!"

The other two took comfort in Jan's words as they walked slowly back toward the stable. "You know, Janny, maybe you're right," Joey said after a moment. "Maybe the treasure wasn't hidden in the walls. It could have been burried under the floor of the tunnel. Next time we search this place, I'm bringing a shovel."

When they reached the trapdoor, they climbed up the stone steps to the stable floor where Inky was waiting for them. He gave a welcoming bark, his tail wagging so hard that half his body wagged along with it.

Heather gathered the little dog up in her arms and hugged him. "You're glad to see me again, aren't you, Inky?" She lingered by the trapdoor and patted his long silky coat. Finally she roused herself. "I guess I'd better be going home. I've been gone a long time and Mom might worry."

"Can you come tomorrow?" asked Jan.

Heather nodded. "I sure will. Wild horses couldn't keep me away!" She looked at Patches and they all laughed.

Jan and Joey walked their new friend across the meadow. They stood on the dock and watched her row across the lake. They kept watching and waving until Aunt Melinda's bell called them for supper.

Mr. Grimes was already seated at the table when they arrived at the kitchen. Aunt Melinda introduced them to the boarder who gave them each a bob of his head in acknowledgment. Before they sat down to eat, Aunt Melinda told Joey to run down to the fruit cellar and get one of the blueberry pies for dessert.

Jan washed her hands and was just taking her place at the table when Joey returned with the pie, but there was a puzzled look on his face.

"There was only one pie down there, Aunt Melinda," he said.

"You must be mistaken, Joey. I know I put two pies in the pie safe this morning."

"Honest. There was just this one pie."

"Well, sit down," Aunt Melinda told him. "After supper I'll go to the fruit cellar and have a look myself."

Joey took his place at the table next to his sister, and Aunt Melinda asked Mr. Grimes if he would say grace. The boarder shook his head, so Aunt Melinda said a short one.

All through the meal, Mr. Grimes hardly spoke two words. *He certainly is a quiet one,* thought Jan. Yet she couldn't help noticing how carefully he listened to what each one of them had to say, his sharp, gray eyes watching them closely as they spoke.

After supper Mr. Grimes retreated to his room and the twins helped Aunt Melinda look for the missing pie.

"The pie safe is empty, all right," Aunt Melinda said when they entered the fruit cellar. "This is the strangest thing ever. I'm sure I baked *two* pies this morning."

"We know you did," Jan said. "Joey and I saw both of them cooling when we came out of the tunnel."

91

Aunt Melinda hesitated then turned to Joey. "Now, young man, you didn't come down here and help yourself to that pie, did you?"

Joey looked shocked. "Of course not, Aunt Melinda. I wouldn't do a thing like that. And if I had, I would have owned up to it by now."

Aunt Melinda smiled and gave his arm a little squeeze. "I believe you, Joey. It's just that I know how much boys like blueberry pie." She looked around the shelves then shook her head. "No use looking anywhere else for it. We all know it was in the pie safe."

She looked more puzzled than ever. "Now what could have happened to it? Pies just don't walk off by themselves." She closed the door to the pie safe and glanced around her again. With another shake of her head, she started back toward the cellar steps.

When they climbed up to the kitchen, they were surprised to find that Mr. Grimes had returned. Aunt Melinda poured him a second cup of coffee and he told her, "I just came back to ask you if you have a boat that I could use on the lake. You see, ma'am, I'd like to do a little fishing."

"There's a rowboat by the dock," Aunt Melinda said. "It's an old one, but I keep it painted and it's watertight. The oars are in the toolshed alongside the barn. They're right inside the door. Feel free to use the boat anytime you like."

"I don't usually fish in the middle of the day," Mr. Grimes mumbled. "Too many kids swimming and boating. Scare the fish. I go out in the evening or at night. Fish bite better then."

92

Joey perked up his ears at what Mr. Grimes was saying. He liked to fish, too, and was hoping that the boarder might ask him to go along. But the somber Mr. Grimes said no more about it. When he finished his coffee, he left the table and went back to his room.

Joey stared after him with a frown. "Boy, he isn't very friendly."

"Maybe he just doesn't like kids," Jan said.

Aunt Melinda began to clear the table. "Now don't bother your heads about him. He seems like a decent enough man and is paying good money for his room. If he wants to be left alone, we won't bother him." Then she said cheerfully, "What do you say tomorrow after church we pack a lunch and have a picnic on the island in the lake? How would you like that?"

"That would be great!" Jan said. "May we ask Heather?"

"Why, of course you may."

Mr. Grimes came down the stairs just then and made his way through the kitchen with his fishing tackle, net, and bait box. Joey walked over to the screen door to watch him get the oars from the toolshed.

"Phew, it's hot," he said. "Let's go swimming, Janny, while it's still light out."

They went to their rooms to change into their bathing suits and a short time later they were having fun splashing in the lake. The water this time of the day was as still and smooth as glass and wonderfully warm, so they swam for quite a while before climbing back on the dock to dry off.

Jan dabbled a toe in the water and watched a school of minnows flash among the rocks. She thought, with a smile, that swimming in White Meadow Lake was just as much fun as swimming in Patty Dawson's new pool.

She squinted across the water and spied Mr. Grimes fishing in a little cove by a wooded island in the middle of the lake. "I wonder if that's the island Aunt Melinda was talking about, where we'll have the picnic tomorrow."

"It must be. It's the only island in the lake." Joey shook his head to get the water out of his ears. "I wonder if Mr. Grimes is catching any fish."

"I'm glad he doesn't like to fish in the middle of the day," Jan said, "or else we couldn't use the boat to get to the island."

"I wonder what he's going to do tomorrow," Joey said.

Jan shrugged. "Who knows? He sure is a funny guy."

Joey sat up on his knees. "Hey, I just had a thought. Maybe he took Aunt Melinda's pie."

Jan giggled. "He doesn't seem like the type who would go around stealing pies."

"Well, then, what became of it?"

Jan sighed. "I don't know. Another mystery, I guess."

She glanced over her shoulder at White Meadow Farm. The sun was going down behind the pines in a splash of red and gold, flinging lavender ribbons

Jan dabbled a toe in the water and watched a school of minnows flash among the rocks.

94

across the sky. The meadow was already shaded in evening grays, and the barn and house were black silhouettes against the mountains.

"There sure are a lot of mysteries around here," she said, half to herself. "Yesterday we heard those creepy footsteps in the barn and last night we saw that strange light crossing the meadow in the storm. Now today it's Aunt Melinda's missing pie."

Joey looked thoughtfully at his sister. "Maybe whoever was in the barn yesterday when we heard those creepy footsteps took the pie. He might have come back today and found it in the fruit cellar."

Jan nodded. "Now that's an idea! Maybe he's that old tramp you thought came to the barn last night to get out of the storm. Maybe he was hungry."

"I don't know who he is, but if he's prowling around inside the tunnel, hunting for the chest of gold, he'd better forget it," Joey said irritably. "It's not his treasure."

"I hope he doesn't come back to search for it while we're on the island tomorrow," Jan said with concern. "I wish we could think of a way to scare him off if he does."

In the next breath she exclaimed, "Joey, I think I know a way!"

"How?"

"We'll keep Inky in the stable. You remember how he barked his head off yesterday when we heard those footsteps."

"Yeah!" Joey said. "Good old Inky will scare him off."

He glanced out across the lake that reflected the red and gold from the sky. With a grin he turned back to his sister. "You know, Janny, with all these mysteries to solve, this vacation might not be such a drag after all!"

8

DISCOVERY ON THE ISLAND

IT WAS BRIGHT and sunny the next morning. A wonderful day for a picnic, Jan thought as she dressed for church. After breakfast Aunt Melinda invited Mr. Grimes to join them. But he refused, saying, in as few words as possible, that he would spend the day reading in his room.

"There are plenty of books in the bookcase in the parlor," Aunt Melinda told him. "You're welcome to help yourself to any one of them."

Mr. Grimes nodded and went into the parlor to

look over the books. Jan was puzzled as she watched him go. Why would Mr. Grimes want to stay in his room with a book on a day like this when he could be outside enjoying himself? Besides, he didn't look at all like the bookworm type. He looked as if he'd much rather be sitting in the sun or fishing or hiking around than reading. Why did he bother coming to White Meadow Lake if he was just going to stay in his room all the time? Jan decided, more than ever, that there was something very strange about Aunt Melinda's border.

Her thoughts were interrupted when her great-aunt called her from the porch. "Come along, Jan, or we'll be late for church."

Aunt Melinda's church was on the other side of the lake. It was a small, white, frame building with long, stained-glass windows and a steeple that blazed white against the deep blue sky. It was just as Jan imagined a country church would look like. The field behind it was filled with cars.

"We have quite a crowd this time of year with all the summer people," Aunt Melinda told them as she edged Bessie between a station wagon and a camper.

The service was very simple, with only six people in the choir and the minister dressed in a plain blue suit. The windows were open and after the hymns were sung, Jan could hear the birds in the maple trees outside and a cow mooing softly in a nearby pasture. She could even see the blue sky and a white fluffy cloud drifting by. It was pleasant going to church in the country, she thought, where you could hear and see God's nature all around you.

After the service, everyone gathered in the churchyard to visit. Pastor Tucker had annouced that there would be a festival on the church grounds tomorrow to raise money for the church, and everyone was busy talking about it. While Aunt Melinda was chattering with some of her friends, Jan and Joey made their way over to where the McNeils were standing.

"Hi!" Heather called out when she saw them. After being introduced to Mr. and Mrs. McNeil, the twins asked Heather if she would like to join them on the picnic.

"Oh, may I go?" Heather begged her parents.

Mrs. McNeil, a plump, friendly-looking woman, smiled at them and nodded. "That would be nice. We're so glad Heather has met some friends her own age." And so it was arranged that they would pick up Heather on their way to the island.

When they got home from church, Jan and Joey quickly changed into comfortable jeans and shirts and helped pack the picnic lunch. Aunt Melinda left some sandwiches, salad, and fruit on the table under a checked tea towel for Mr. Grimes.

Inky waited by the door, watching all the preparations with eager eyes and wagging tail. Aunt Melinda looked down at the little dog with concern. "He wants to go but there will be too many of us in the rowboat, so I'll have to shut him in the house. I hope he won't bark when we leave and bother Mr. Grimes."

"Why not put Inky in the barn?" Joey suggested quickly, giving his sister a knowing glance. "If he barks there, he won't bother Mr. Grimes."

"All right, Joey, take him to the barn. Jan, bring his bowl and fill it with water and we'll leave a few dog biscuits for him."

The twins opened the screen door and headed for the barn, the unsuspecting Inky close at their heels.

"You're going to guard the stable today," Jan told the little dog as she placed the dish of water and biscuits in the corner near the trapdoor. "It's a very important job, so be on your best guard."

Inky cocked his head in a puzzled way when they started to leave without him.

"I feel terrible, leaving him behind like this," Jan said as she listened to the dog's pleading whines on the other side of the stable door. They left the top half of the door open so that the stable wouldn't be so dark.

"You said yourself it's the only way to guard the tunnel while we're gone," Joey reminded her. "Anyway, you heard what Aunt Melinda said. There would be no room for him in the boat."

Aunt Melinda came out of the house just then. She looked quite gay in a bright gingham sunbonnet, the big picnic basket swinging on her arm. After Joey got the oars from the toolshed, they started across the meadow.

"Do you know how to row?" Aunt Melinda asked as she watched Joey put the oars into the oarlocks.

"Sure. I learned at camp." Joey held the boat close to the dock so that Jan and Aunt Melinda could step in.

Aunt Melinda sat on the wide stern seat and Jan hopped into the bow so that she could untie the rope that held the boat. Joey took the seat between the oars and after Jan had untied the painter, he shoved off.

He raised the oars and dipped them. He was used to aluminum boats and this old wooden rowboat seemed awkward to maneuver at first; but soon, after a bit of splashing and tugging, he was pulling at the oars in a sure, steady rhythm and they were moving across the lake.

A breeze had sprung up, throwing sunlit ripples across the blue water.

"My, look how the lake sparkles!" Aunt Melinda exclaimed. "It always does on a bright sunny day."

Joey pointed the prow of the boat toward the line of docks on the far side of the lake. It wasn't difficult to find the McNeil dock. Heather was standing at the end of it, waving to them.

Joey stopped rowing and let the boat drift until it bumped gently against the rubber tires lined as a buffer alongside the dock. Heather stepped into the boat and sat down on the stern seat next to Aunt Melinda.

Aunt Melinda straightened her sunbonnet and smiled at the girl. "Nice you can be with us, Heather."

"I brought a choclate cake Mom made," Heather said, glancing down at the cake tin she held on her lap.

Joey couldn't take his eyes off the cake tin. "Hmmm, chocolate's my favorite kind of cake!" he said, running his tongue around the edge of his lips and rolling his eyes upward in delight.

Aunt Melinda laughed and called out, "Watch

where you're going, young man, or you'll miss the island."

Joey pulled hard on his left oar and swung the boat around in the right direction. He kept his mind on his rowing until they reached the island.

Aunt Melinda directed him to a small cove with a sandy beach and Joey ran the prow of the boat up on the smooth sand. They all got out and Jan tied the boat to a stout willow branch that hung over the water.

"This is where we usually picnic," Aunt Melinda said as she led the way to a grassy clearing up from the beach. "It's too boggy and full of brush in the center of the island."

"Can we eat now?" Joey asked eagerly. "I'm famished."

Aunt Melinda spread a plastic tablecloth on the grass and the girls helped her unpack the picnic basket. They drew out a bowl of potato salad, a plate of deviled eggs, a jar of pickles, and the sandwiches wrapped in aluminum foil. For dessert Heather displayed her mother's choclate cake, iced with thick white frosting.

"Well, it doesn't look as if we'll starve," Jan laughed as she viewed all the food.

Heather bit into one of Aunt Melinda's chicken salad sandwiches. "Hmmm, this is super!"

"Aunt Melinda's the best cook in the world," Joey boasted, his mouth full of deviled egg. Aunt Melinda's eyes twinkled at her great-nephew's praise.

"It's fun eating on an island in the middle of the lake," Jan mused. "What a pretty sight our white meadow is from here."

"This is the month every weed and wild flower is blooming," Aunt Melinda told them. "I don't know why some folks don't like weeds that flower. I think our Queen Anne's lace is just as pretty as any rose."

"I think so too," Heather agreed. "I just love to make bouquets out of Queen Anne's lace and blue chicory and wild asters." Then she added, "Oh, look, there's Patches by the barn."

"Wow, you can see everything from here," Joey exclaimed, "the house and the barn and everything."

The children kept munching their sandwiches and staring across the lake. They didn't notice the small canoe that drifted into view around the end of the island. And the boy in the canoe was too busy fishing to notice them.

When the canoe drifted closer to shore, Aunt Melinda looked up suddenly and said, "Why, there's Jim Eagle, Trader Dan's son. I haven't seen him since his father was taken to the hospital."

The children swung around and stared curiously at the boy in the canoe. His face was brown and angular, with high cheekbones, and his straight black hair hung down almost to his shoulders.

"Jim Eagle?" Joey asked in a low voice. "That's a funny name."

"Jim is a native American Indian," Aunt Melinda informed them. "His father, Dan Eagle, runs a service station. Their station is down by the inlet. This summer Dan took sick and has to be in the hospital for a long time. Jim has no mother, so his uncle from New Mexico was to come East to take Jim back with him to live on the reservation. I'm surprised to see that Jim is still here."

Aunt Melinda laid down her sandwich and called, "Jim! Jim Eagle! Come and have some lunch with us."

The boy in the canoe started. Quickly he drew in his line and looked at them with wary eyes. Joey watched him eagerly. It would be great to have a real Indian boy for a friend. He hoped Jim Eagle would paddle in to shore.

But Jim Eagle kept his distance and looked at them with narrow eyes that seemed both surprised and unfriendly. Quickly he put his pole down and reached for his paddle. Before Aunt Melinda could call to him again, he had paddled out of sight around the tip of the island.

"Well, I declare," Aunt Melinda said mildly. "Jim Eagle certainly does act strange. It's not like him to paddle off like that without even speaking. He's always been such a polite, friendly boy."

"He sure doesn't seem friendly to me," Joey said with disappointment.

"Well, maybe he's worried about his father in the hospital," Aunt Melinda said. "I wonder when that uncle of his is coming."

Heather passed dessert around and soon the strange-acting boy was forgotten as they bit into the delicious chocolate cake with creamy frosting. After they had finished eating, Joey said, "Let's explore the island."

"Let's!" the girls chorused.

"You go on and have fun," Aunt Melinda told them. "I think I'll stay right here and rest and enjoy the cool breeze."

105

Joey started forward and the girls followed him through the tall grass and bushes toward the center of the island. They hadn't gone far when Heather called out, "Look at the wild grapevine hanging down from this tree. It'd make a neat swing."

They tugged at the vine to see if it would hold them, then they took turns swinging on it. "Me Tarzan," Joey called out when it was his turn and he was swinging back and forth in front of them.

Jan laughed. "Oh, come on. Let's see what else we can find."

They explored the bog in the middle of the island and watched minnows and tadpoles swimming back and forth in the dark water.

While they were watching the tiny fish a shadow passed overhead and when they looked up, they saw wide wings sailing over them.

"Look!" Jan breathed as a large bird lighted on the other side of the bog and stood poised on its long, stilted legs in the shallow water, watching them.

"It's a blue heron," Heather said.

For a long while they watched the heron until it thrust out its crooked neck, unfolded its large, graceful wings, and flew around the bog, skimming over the dark water and finally dipping down on the very top of the tallest hemlock. There it perched, a silent sentinel, keeping watch over the island.

"You'd never know a heron was on top of that tree unless you saw it land there," Joey said, taking another look at the dark, shadowy bird in the foliage of the hemlock. "I never knew a heron could perch in the very top of a tree. What keeps it up there?"

"Perfect balance, I guess," Heather said. "There are lots of blue herons on the lake. Daddy says they like to nest along quiet, shallow water."

"I never knew they could fly so gracefully," Jan said, not taking her eyes off the top of the tall hemlock. "I've got to tell Patty Dawson about it when we get home."

When it looked as though the heron wasn't going to leave its perch in the treetop, they decided to move on. They jumped from one grassy tussock to another until they reached dry ground again. It was then that they stumbled upon a narrow path leading back through the trees.

"I wonder where it goes," Heather said.

Joey waved the girls on. "Let's follow it and find out." They followed the winding trace to a grove of hemlocks on the far end of the island. In the center of the grove, almost hidden from sight, was an open space.

Joey stopped suddenly and glanced down at the ground. Only a few feet away were the charred remains of a campfire. He bent over to look at the burned logs. But it wasn't the remains of the campfire that Jan was staring at. It was a shiny object on a flat rock next to the burned log that had caught her eye. She ran over to pick it up.

"Look at this!"

When Joey saw what she was holding, he called back, "So what? It's just an aluminum pie pan. Someone like us probably ate their lunch on this island."

"But *look* at it," Jan demanded.

Puzzled, Joey walked over to where his sister was standing, and when he saw the blue stain around the rim, he exclaimed, "Blueberry pie!"

"Do you think it could have been Aunt Melinda's missing pie?" Jan asked. "It looks like one of her pie pans."

"A missing pie!" laughed Heather. "I've heard of missing persons and missing pets before but never missing pies."

When Jan told her about the strange disappearance of the blueberry pie yesterday, Heather eyed the pan with a puzzled frown. "But how could one of your aunt's pies get way over here on the island? It doesn't make sense."

"Well, somebody could have brought it over here to eat," reasoned Jan.

Joey kicked at an empty bean can and sent it rolling across the charred remains of the fire. "But we're not sure it's Aunt Melinda's," he declared. "It could be somebody else's blueberry pie that was brought here for their picnic."

"Picnickers don't usually go off and leave their good aluminum pie pans behind," Jan protested. "Mom wouldn't do that."

"Okay, let's show it to Aunt Melinda," Joey decided. "If it's not hers, we can bring it back here again."

The three of them cut back across the island. They edged their way around the bog, glancing up at the tallest hemlock to see if the heron was still perched on the top. But it must have flown off, for it wasn't there that they could see. They hurried on past the swinging grapevine and when they returned to the sandy beach, they found Aunt Melinda leaning against a log with her eyes closed. She sat up with a start at the sudden, noisy intrusion of the children.

"Back so soon?" she asked.

Without wasting words, Jan thrust the pie pan in front of her great-aunt and said breathlessly, "Look what we found."

Aunt Melinda seemed interested. She took the pie pan from Jan and turned it upside down so that she could examine it. "Why this is one of mine!" she exclaimed.

"Are you sure?" the three of them asked in shrill voices.

"Of course I'm sure. See, here on the bottom is where I always scratch my initials. I bake pies for so many church suppers that I always mark my pans this way so that I'm sure to get the right ones back."

They peered over Aunt Melinda's shoulder and stared at the thin initials, *M. H.* that were scratched on the bottom of the pan.

"Wow-ee!" exclaimed Joey. "I'll bet it had the missing blueberry pie in it."

Aunt Melinda looked puzzled. "What's it doing here on the island? Where did you find it?"

Quickly they told her about finding the remains of the campfire at the far end of the island and the pie pan on a flat rock alongside it. Joey was about to tell her about finding the empty bean can that was evidence that somebody had been eating on the island when the faint, muffled barking of a dog

109

sounded across the lake. There was something familiar about the dog's barking. They stopped talking at once and listened.

"Hey, isn't that Inky!" cried Joey.

They all turned to stare at White Meadow Farm across the way, and at the same moment Jan grasped her brother's arm and pointed.

"Look!" she said in a hoarse whisper as she glimpsed the figure of a man emerging from the barn. "Isn't that Mr. Grimes?"

9

MR. GRIMES' STRANGE ACTIONS

JOEY SHADED his eyes with his hand as he peered across the lake. "It sure is Mr. Grimes," he said. "I wonder what he was doing in our barn."

"Well, he's not spending his afternoon reading, that's for sure!" declared Jan.

The children exchanged puzzled glances.

Aunt Melinda got up and reached for her sunbonnet. "We'd better be starting back. Maybe he wants something."

Ordinarily the children would have been reluctant to start back so soon, but now they leaped to action. Joey untied the boat while the girls helped Aunt Melinda gather up the picnic things. When they were all in the boat, Joey dipped the oars deep into the water and in no time at all they were on their way across the lake.

When they had reached the dock and made sure the boat was securely tied, they gathered their belongings and started across the meadow. By the time they reached the barn, Mr. Grimes was nowhere in sight.

Inky started barking again when he heard them coming. Joey opened the stable door and the cocker spaniel fairly flew out at them. He jumped around them as if he were on springs, happily sniffing their feet and whining with ecstasy.

"Wow, nobody was ever this happy to see me before," Joey said, reaching over and giving the little dog a pat.

"That's a dog for you," Aunt Melinda answered. "Man's best friend."

"And woman's, too," Jan added, giving Inky an extra pat.

Joey remained in the yard to play with Inky and Aunt Melinda and the girls went into the house. Aunt Melinda wasted no time in heading for the stairs and the curious girls hurried after her. They stood quietly in the upstairs hallway while she tapped gently on Mr. Grimes' door.

"Is there anything you want, Mr. Grimes?" Aunt Melinda asked.

"No—no," came a muffled reply from behind the closed door.

"We were picnicking on the island and saw you coming out of the barn. We wondered if you were looking for something," Aunt Melinda went on.

There was a moment's hesitation behind the door. Then Mr. Grimes' voice replied, "I was just looking for a shovel—to dig some night crawlers for fishing tonight."

"Well my land," laughed Aunt Melinda, "that shovel is not in the barn. It's in the toolshed."

"Yes, yes, I know, Miss Howard," came the impatient reply from behind the closed door. "I found it. Now I would like to finish by book."

Without another word they turned away and went downstairs.

"Boy, what a grump," Heather exclaimed under her breath when they were in the kitchen again.

"I know!" Jan whispered back.

The girls got cold drinks from the refrigerator and Aunt Melinda sat down in the rocker by the window with the Sunday paper. After they finished their drinks, Heather said, "Let's go outside and ride Patches."

Joey was still in the yard, throwing sticks for Inky to retrieve. When he saw the girls coming out of the house, he gave up playing with the little dog and followed them to the barnyard gate where Patches was nickering for attention.

"Did Aunt Melinda find out what Mr. Grimes was doing in the barn?" he asked as they led the pinto into the stable to bridle and saddle her.

"He told Aunt Melinda he was hunting for a shovel to dig worms," Jan informed him.

Joey made a wry face. "That sounds suspicious to

113

me. You'd think he'd look in the toolshed for a shovel."

"That's where Aunt Melinda told him it was," replied Jan.

Joey helped Heather lift the heavy saddle onto Patches' back while Jan took the lines down from a wooden peg along the wall.

Patches bent her head obligingly as Jan slipped the harness over her head and ears. She fastened the lead reins to the halter rings, tossed them over the horse's neck, and they led Patches out of the stable.

"You ride first, Jan," Heather offered after she had fixed the stirrups and made sure the saddle girth was tight enough.

Jan mounted, gathered the reins in her hands, and rode out of the barnyard and down the lane. Patches cantered smoothly at first and then she was trotting. Jan's long, sandy-colored hair flew out and her blue eyes sparkled with excitement. After trotting up and down the road several times, she reined in her mount by the stable gate.

"Who wants to ride next?" She slid off Patches' back and held the pinto while Heather mounted.

"Wow, she sure can ride," Joey said with admiration as they watched Heather put Patches through her gaits. Then it was his turn.

Joey wished that he could show off his riding ability as well as the girls, but he had to admit that they were both better riders than he.

Oh well, baseball is my favorite sport," he consoled himself as he rode up and down the road in a cantering gait.

114

After their rides Joey led Patches into her stall and the girls got busy rubbing her down. When they finished, they let her browse in the meadow.

"Now what can we do?" Jan wondered.

"Let's show Heather the secret room," Joey suggested. "We can go back to the house through the hidden tunnel."

"We don't have your flashlight," Jan reminded him.

"Oh yes we do," Joey said, reaching for his flashlight on the shelf next to the saddle soap. "I'm keeping it here now so I don't have to keep running to my room for it."

They opened the trapdoor and one by one descended the stone steps leading into the dark passageway. It wasn't nearly as spooky today as it had been the first time they had come to explore. Joey walked ahead, swinging his flashlight back and forth confidently.

"Don't go so fast," Heather called out. "I'm the last one and I don't want to get lost."

"Lost!" snorted Joey. "You can't get lost in this tunnel." And with that he went even faster. Squealing with excitement, the girls hurried after him. They were almost through the tunnel when Joey stopped so suddenly that the girls almost fell over him.

"What's the matter?" Jan called out. "Why are you stopping?"

Joey was too speechless to answer. He was staring down at a pile of loose ground on the earthen floor of the tunnel. Next to it was a deep hole. Peering over his shoulder, the girls spied the hole, too.

115

Jan sucked in her breath. "This wasn't here the last time we were in the tunnel."

"It looks as if somebody was digging here," Heather observed.

Joey nodded grimly. "Somebody's been here since we were here last. That's for sure."

They looked at one another in the dim glow of the flashlight. Then in one voice they breathed, "Mr. Grimes!"

Joey frowned. "The hidden tunnel sure is a funny place to be digging for worms!"

"Maybe he was hunting for the lost treasure," Heather whispered.

"But why would Mr. Grimes be hunting for the treasure?" Jan tried to reason. "He's a stranger around here and couldn't have known about the treasure or the tunnel. Even we didn't know until we read about them in Martha Howard's diary."

She stopped talking suddenly and stared at the other two. "That's it!" she gasped. "Mr. Grimes could have read about them in the diary."

"How could he?" asked Joey. "He doesn't know about the diary."

"But maybe he does," Jan said. "Remember what Aunt Melinda told him before we went to church this morning? She told him to help himself to any books in the bookcase."

"Yeah, I remember," Joey said slowly, "but what does that have to do with the diary?"

"Well, I saw Aunt Melinda put it on the top shelf of the bookcase the day Mr. Larson called and you went to the door to let him in," Jan rushed on. "I'll bet she forgot she had put it there when she told

116

Mr. Grimes this morning that he could read any book he wanted to."

"Oh wow!" Joey wailed. "And that diary tells all about the hidden tunnel and the lost treasure."

The twins looked so unhappy and worried that Heather suggested, "Let's go back to the house and see if the diary is in the bookcase. It might still be there and Mr. Grimes hasn't found it at all."

"He must have found it," Jan cried in a desperate voice, "or how would he know to dig in this tunnel?"

Joey's eyes were shadowed in thought. "Wait a minute, Janny," he said slowly. "It could have been someone else. Remember those footsteps we heard the day we were playing in the hayloft? Someone besides Mr. Grimes knows about this tunnel."

Jan gave her brother a concerned look. "I remember. Well, let's see if the diary's still in the bookcase. If it is, then that leaves out Mr. Grimes."

They stepped around the pile of dirt and hurried on through the tunnel. They wasted no time in making their way through the fruit cellar and up the steps to the kitchen.

Aunt Melinda was still absorbed in her Sunday paper and didn't seem to notice them as they slipped past her and into the empty parlor. They went directly to the bookcase. Breathlessly, Jan opened the glass doors and her eyes flew to the top shelf of books.

"It's not here!" she exclaimed softly, looking around her in bewilderment. "I'm sure Aunt Melinda put it on this shelf."

They examined all the books on the top shelf carefully, but the diary wasn't among them.

117

"Maybe it's on one of the other shelves," Heather suggested.

They searched the other shelves, too, and even reached way back behind the books, but they couldn't find the old leather-bound diary anywhere.

At last they gave up their search and glanced at one another with troubled eyes.

"The diary is gone!" Jan whispered in a low, accusing tone.

Joey sat back on his heels, his face clouded with worry.

"Oh boy! That means Mr. Grimes could have found it this morning while he was looking for a book to read. He could have read it while we were at church and found out about the treasure in the tunnel."

The girls nodded grimly.

"I wish we could search his room," Joey went on in a low voice. "If we could and found the diary there, then we'd know for sure that he was the one digging in the tunnel."

"Oh, Joey, you know Aunt Melinda would never let us search his room," Jan said. "Besides, it wouldn't be right to snoop in his things behind his back."

Just then they heard their great-aunt moving about in the kitchen. Quickly they closed the glass doors of the bookcase and sped like flying shadows up the two flights of stairs to the attic.

10

THE MISSING DIARY

AFTER THEY showed Heather the secret room and the old chest where Joey had found the diary, the girls couldn't resist playing dress-up. While they were trying on some of the old dresses and hats, Joey sat on the cot against the chimney wall, his chin resting on his hand, deep in thought.

"There are some mighty peculiar things going on around here," he spoke his thoughts aloud. "Let's go over the mysteries again and try to figure out some of them."

Jan pushed a floppy, plumed hat back on her head and rolled her eyes upward. "Okay. Let's see. There is the mystery of the lost treasure. That's the most important one of all. We still don't have that one solved."

"Then we heard those footsteps in the barn," Joey added, "and we think the prowler hid in the tunnel because the bale of straw was moved. Boy, I wish we could have searched the tunnel right then and there. We could have caught him."

"But Aunt Melinda rang her bell for us," Jan explained to Heather, "and we had to go."

"What was the next mystery?" Heather wanted to know. She stepped out of the high heels she was wearing, tossed them back into the trunk, and came over to sit on the cot next to Joey. Jan took off the floppy hat and laid it on top of the other things in the old trunk. Playing dress-up was soon forgotten as the three huddled together in the secret room to discuss the mysteries.

"Let's see." Joey screwed his eyes up in a thoughtful way. "Oh yeah, it was Aunt Melinda's missing pie."

"And finding that pie on the island," Jan added.

"I'll bet the prowler in the barn took the pie," Heather said, hoping to lend some light to the mystery.

"He must have," Jan reasoned, "but who is he and what was he doing eating Aunt Melinda's pie on the island?"

"Sounds wild, really way out in left field," Joey said with a thin laugh. Then he added, "Don't forget

120

the light we saw in the meadow during the storm."

"That's the most scary thing of all," Jan remembered, "because Martha Howard mentioned a light in the meadow in her diary and wrote that it was the ghost of Amos Brown returning to the barn to escape the sheriff. He was shot and died in the stable."

"Of course we don't believe in ghosts," Joey quickly reminded her, "and Aunt Melinda said she never saw the ghost in all the years she's lived here. Still, it's a mystery why anyone would be wandering across the meadow in a stormy night."

Heather heaved a deep sigh. "And now the mysterious person who was digging in the tunnel and the missing diary," she said, bringing the mysteries up to date. "They seem to point to Mr. Grimes."

"They sure do," agreed Joey. "I wish we could search his room. I'll just bet we'd find that diary."

The three of them lapsed into silence, each one thinking his own thoughts about the mysteries, when the dinner bell pealed out from below. The sound of it in the quiet attic made them jump. They leaped up from the cot and hurried out of the secret room. After carefully closing the wall paneling, they went down the stairs where Aunt Melinda was waiting for them on the bottom landing.

"Heather's mother telephoned and wants her home," Aunt Melinda announced. "Joey, suppose you row Heather across the lake."

"May I go, too?" Jan asked.

"Yes, but be sure you both come right back for supper."

Joey rowed the girls across the lake to the McNeil

dock. As Heather stepped out of the boat, she said, "If it's okay, I'll row over first thing in the morning."

"Yeah. Sure thing," Joey said as he pushed the boat away from the dock. They waved goodbye to their friend and started back across the lake. They were passing the end of the island by the grove of hemlocks when Jan glimpsed a canoe half hidden under the dark trees that hung over the water.

At first the canoe seemed empty, but as she stared at it, she noticed somebody bent over in it. She looked closely and exclaimed in a low voice, "Joey, there's Jim Eagle watching us."

Joey let the oars drift and swung around to see where his sister was pointing. When he spied the familiar dark figure, he called out in a friendly voice, "Hi!"

The boy jerked up and reached for his paddle.

"Hey, wait a minute," Joey called. "My name's Joey Howard and this is my sister Jan. Our aunt said you're Jim Eagle."

The Indian boy scowled at Joey, then started pushing the canoe out from under the hemlocks.

"Would you like to go fishing sometime?" Joey tried again.

Jim Eagle shook his head, still scowling.

"Why not?" Joey persisted.

This time Jim answered him. "Because I want to fish alone, that's why."

"Okay, if you want to," Joey said in a disappointed voice, "but how about coming over to our farm sometime. We can have a lot of fun playing in my aunt's barn."

At the mention of the barn, Jim stared at Joey with eyes that seemed both angry and frightened. "That old barn is haunted," he called back in a rough voice. "A man was shot and died in there a long time ago. That's no place to play."

And with that, he hastily paddled away from the island.

Joey was so shocked and disappointed at the boy's strange, unfriendly behavior that for a moment he just sat staring after the departing canoe. Then he became angry.

"Oh great!" he yelled after Jim Eagle. "Don't tell me you believe in ghosts!"

The boy didn't bother to reply. He kept paddling rapidly toward the inlet.

Jan shifted uneasily on her seat. "Come on, Joey," she urged, "let's get home."

Joey grabbed the oars roughly and rowed on past the island. "Ghosts!" he muttered. "That's a laugh. That guy can go to his uncle's reservation in New Mexico for all I care. I'm not going to bother with him anymore!"

Supper was a silent affair that night. Mr. Grimes said nothing at all; Joey was still brooding about the unfriendly Jim Eagle; and Aunt Melinda, herself, seemed pensive.

She's probably thinking about the mortgage money and that White Meadow Farm might not belong to the Howards much longer, Jan thought. Then Jan herself began to feel depressed. They had searched the tunnel thoroughly but they were no closer to finding the lost treasure than they had been in the beginning. And now someone else was hunting for it, too.

If it weren't for the diary telling that Great-Great-Great-Grandfather John Howard had put the chest of gold in the hidden tunnel, I wouldn't think it was there at all, Jan told herself as she toyed with her dessert.

After supper Mr. Grimes left the table and went to his room.

When he came down a short time later, he was carrying his fishing pole and tackle box. Without a word he started for the lake.

Joey, lounging in the swing on the back porch, stared moodily across the meadow after the departing fisherman. Jan sat down on the swing next to her brother and Aunt Melinda came out on the porch and drew up a rocker.

"What's the matter, Joey?" she asked, coming right to the point, "You have been brooding all through supper."

Joey told her about their encounter with Jim Eagle that afternoon after they had taken Heather home. "Some guy!" he ended. "He sure is unfriendly."

Aunt Melinda rocked steadily, rhythmically. Then she said, "It's strange that Jim should be acting like that. He has always been a friendly boy. Have you thought that maybe there is a reason why he's acting the way he does?"

Joey stopped swinging and looked across at his great-aunt. "What do you mean?" he asked. "What reason does he have to act like that? I didn't do anything to him."

"I know you didn't; still, a person doesn't act that way unless there is a reason," Aunt Melinda said. "Maybe with some kindness and understanding, you can find what that reason is."

"Well, I'm not going to try," Joey said stubbornly. "I don't care how he acts from now on."

"That's too bad," Aunt Melinda went on. "Jim would make a good friend for you to play with, Joey. I can't help but think that there's something troubling that boy."

Aunt Melinda rocked in silence for a while longer then got up. "I might as well get started on my errand," she said. "Mrs. Bronson, who lives on the next farm, offered me some of her baking apples to make pies for the church festival. I better go for them before it gets too late. Want to ride along?"

"I guess not," Joey said moodily and Jan decided not to go either.

"Well, I won't be gone long," Aunt Melinda told them. She went into the house for her sweater and a container for the apples. When she came out on the porch again, she had a letter in her hand. "Dear me, the mailman brought a letter yesterday for Mr. Grimes and I forgot to give it to him. Would you two run it up to his room and put it on his dresser? That's where we agreed I'd put his mail."

Joey snapped out of his dark mood. "Sure thing," he answered quickly, throwing a meaningful glance at his sister.

Jan understood his look and returned it with her eyes gleaming. With this letter as an excuse, what a wonderful opportunity to get into Mr. Grimes' room and look around for the missing diary!

Aunt Melinda handed them the letter and scurried off on her errand. They watched while she got the car out of the garage. When at last Bessie came groaning up the lane, they waved and when the old car was out of sight, they slid off the swing and dashed into the house.

Like two spies they stole up the front stairs. The house seemed quiet and empty with no grown-ups in it. The hallway was already dim with shadows. A little shivery feeling crept down Jan's spine and she held her breath when Joey put his hand on Mr. Grimes' doorknob.

The knob turned slowly and the door creaked open.

"What luck!" Joey whispered as if the walls of the old house had ears. "Now that we're here, we can take a look around."

The twins peered into the big front bedroom. Fortunately its two windows faced west and there was enough daylight left so that they didn't have to turn on the light. They stood in the middle of the room, like guilty intruders, and glanced around at Mr. Grimes' personal belongings.

The room was tidy. The boarder's traveling bag was in the corner by the door. His good suit of clothes was hanging in the wardrobe. A road map lay unfolded on top of the dresser, but everything else seemed to be in perfect order. Jan walked over to the dresser and placed the letter next to the map.

Joey was examining several books that were piled neatly on a little maple table by the window. His eyes quickly scanned their covers. They were books Mr. Grimes had borrowed from Aunt Melinda's bookcase but the old leather-bound diary was not one of them.

Jan gazed curiously around the room—to the bed, the dresser, and to the mahogany chest of drawers next to the wardrobe. There were no more books in sight. She drew a deep sigh. "I don't see the diary anywhere. We'd better leave now."

But Joey wasn't ready to give up yet. Boldly he walked over to the chest of drawers and drew open the top drawer. Jan caught her breath.

"Joey, you shouldn't be prying into Mr. Grimes' personal belongings!"

"If he took the diary and didn't want anybody to know he has it, he wouldn't keep it out in the open, would he?" Joey explained, defending his actions. He went on searching the drawer.

"Be sure you leave his things just as you found them," Jan warned, "or he'll know somebody's been in his room."

"Okay, okay, Miss Fussy. Now help me search."

Jan had a guilty feeling as she looked through the bottom drawer. It didn't take long because Mr. Grimes didn't have that many clothes. They both searched the middle drawer then glanced about the room again. Joey got down on his hands and knees and looked under the bed while Jan opened the little drawer of the bed table. It was empty except for an old Bible with a faded cover that Aunt Melinda must have kept there for years.

Next they searched the wardrobe. They looked on the shelf and squeezed into the farthest end and felt around in each dark corner, but the diary wasn't there either.

"He just doesn't have it," Jan declared at last. "We've searched all through his room and it's not here."

Joey peeked under the corners of the mattress and felt under the pillow. Then he said with a sigh,

"I guess you're right, Janny. But where can it be?"

They turned toward the door and were about to leave the room when Jan's gaze fell on the unfolded map lying across the dresser. On impulse she walked over to the dresser and lifted the map. Underneath it were Mr. Grimes' key ring and—

"Oh-hh," she breathed as she glanced down at the leather-bound diary.

Joey leaped across the room to where she was standing. "Oh wow!" he exploded. "It was right here on top of this dresser."

With trembling fingers Jan opened the diary, turning its pages. "Look, Joey, he's been reading it. This paper marker wasn't stuck between these pages the last time we looked at it."

She glanced down at the words written on the marked pages and sucked in her breath with a faint hiss.

Joey peered over her shoulder and squinted at Martha Howard's thin, spidery writing. He glimpsed the words "Elias Henry"--"chest of gold coins"--and "in the hidden tunnel."

"Phew-ee," he whistled softly. "That proves that Mr. Grimes found the tunnel and was digging there for the treasure."

No sooner had he spoken than a loud creak sounded from the stairs. They stared at one another with alarm. Then there was another creak and another one.

Jan felt a quick, hot throb of fear in her chest. In a voice that was a tiny squeak, she gasped, "Someone's coming!"

Quickly they replaced the diary underneath the map. "Let's get out of here!" Joey whispered.

But it was too late. Soft, hurried footfalls were coming down the dark hallway. They were headed in the direction of Mr. Grimes' room.

11

THE FESTIVAL

"SHUT THE door! Shut the door!" Jan hissed with alarm.

Joey leaped for the door. But before he had a chance to close it, a happy whine and two short barks greeted him from the dark hall. The next moment a wagging tail banged against his leg.

"Inky!" they both cried at once.

The little cocker spaniel came into the room and ran circles around them. Joey grabbed him and hugged him. "Man, did you give us a scare, fella!"

Inky wiggled in the boy's arms and licked his face.

"We better get out of here," Jan warned. After that scare she didn't want to stay in this room a minute longer.

Joey lingered in the doorway. "Do you suppose we should tell Aunt Melinda about Mr. Grimes' reading the diary?"

Jan thought a minute then shook her head. "She has enough to worry about. We'll just have to keep an eagle eye on Mr. Grimes from now on. We'll watch every move he makes. Now let's get going."

They cast a final, quick glance back at the room to make certain that they had left everything just as it was, then closed the door and hurried down the dark hallway with Inky still in Joey's arms. By the time they reached the back porch, they saw old Bessie turning into the lane.

Aunt Melinda was full of enthusiasm on her return. "It's going to be the best church festival ever," she told them. "The high school band is going to play this year. And guess what? Mr. Bronson told me that there will be pony rides for the young people. He's in charge of the rides and asked if you two would like to help him."

"Oh, that would be fun!" exclaimed Jan, leaping up from the swing and helping Aunt Melinda carry the basket of apples into the kitchen as if nothing had happened while she was away.

The next morning early Aunt Melinda started on her apples pies. Heather appeared at the kitchen door even before the twins had finished their breakfast. They were so anxious to tell her about finding the diary in Mr. Grimes' room that they finished the rest of their breakfast as fast as they could. As soon as the dishes were done, the three fled to the stable where they could talk.

Heather was as excited as they about finding the diary. "What are you going to do now that Mr. Grimes knows about the lost treasure?" she asked. "Suppose he finds it first?"

"We're going to keep an eye on him," Joey assured her. "We'll watch every move he makes from now on."

"And that shouldn't be too hard," Jan added, "because he's in his room most of the time."

"But what about tonight?" Heather asked. "Aren't you going to the church festival?"

The twins exchanged startled glances. They hadn't thought about that.

"Yeah, that's right," Joey said with concern in his blue eyes. "Suppose while we're all at the festival he gets lucky and finds the treasure?"

An uneasy feeling crept over Jan. *It could just happen,* she had to admit to herself. She sank down on the bale of straw over the trapdoor. Resting her chin in her hands, she tried to put her thoughts into some kind of order. As she did so, and idea popped into her head.

It was such a tremedous idea that she leaped up excitedly. *Why,* she thought, *hasn't it occurred to me before!*

"Let Mr. Grimes dig in the tunnel all he wants tonight," she exclaimed. "If he does find the treasure, he won't be able to get away with it."

Joey and Heather stared at her, wide-eyed.

"Why won't he?" they asked.

"Because we'll have his car keys!" Jan told them, triumphantly.

"What!" Joey fairly shouted the word at her.

Jan held up her hand for him to calm down and listen. "Last night when we were looking for the diary, I noticed his ring of car keys on the dresser under the map," she explained. "If we could get his keys and hide them tonight, he'd have no way to leave White Meadow Farm with the treasure—if he should find it."

"And how are we going to get the keys if he's in his room all day?" Joey was still skeptical about her plan.

"That's easy," Jan went on to explain. "When he comes down for lunch, we can make an excuse to leave the table for a minute and slip up into his room and get them. We can quickly hide them in one of our rooms, then hurry back to the table."

"But what if he discovers they're gone?" Joey asked, shaking his head doubtfully.

"He'd probably think he just mislaid them," Heather said with a giggle. "I think Jan's idea is a good one."

"And first thing tomorrow we can slip them back to his room during breakfast," Jan said finally. "Maybe he won't even miss them in that short period of time."

Joey thought a minute longer about Jan's idea, then his face broke into a grin. "And you thought it was so terrible to search through his chest of drawers for the diary!"

133

Jan sat up, her cheeks flushed. "Well, if he's being sneaky and digging in the tunnel for the lost treasure, I don't see anything wrong with stopping him from getting away if he should find it!"

Joey was still grinning. "Yeah, as nutty as it sounds, Janny, your idea might not be so bad after all. And maybe he'll be so busy hunting for those keys tonight, he'll forget all about hunting for the treasure."

"Then it's settled," Jan said. "We'll get them this noon. It's our only chance if we're going to have supper at the festival tonight."

"I'll get them," offered Joey, but Jan shook her head. "He wouldn't suspect a girl as much as he would a boy. And, besides," she added nobly, "if anybody should get caught hiding his keys, it should be me because it was my idea in the first place."

After that was settled, Heather got up and reached for the currycomb. "Mr. Bronson asked if he could borrow Patches for the older children to ride at the festival," she told them, "and Daddy said it would be okay. Mr. Bronson has a horse trailer and is coming here for Patches this morning, so I better get her groomed."

"We'll help you," Jan offered eagerly. It would be good to be kept busy. The morning would pass quickly that way, and lunchtime, when her plan to hide Mr. Grimes' keys could be put into action, wouldn't seem so far off.

With currycomb and brush they started working on the pinto. They brushed her spotted coat until it shone. They combed her tangled mane and tail until

134

they hung straight and silky. They polished her hoofs and her saddle and bridle. When they finished their grooming, they stood back to admire their work.

"She looks great," Joey exclaimed.

"She'll be the star of the festival," Jan added triumphantly.

As if she knew what they were saying, Patches nodded and whinnied at her admirers.

"You vain old thing!" Heather laughed, giving the pinto a playful slap on the rump.

Joey suggested they keep Patches in her stall so that she wouldn't get dirty, and to keep her contented, he put some oats in her feedbox. Then they went up to the porch to wait for Mr. Bronson.

His red and white horse van arrived just before noon. In the flurry of helping Mr. Bronson get Patches to the festival, everyone forgot about the conspiracy to take Mr. Grimes' keys. Everyone but Jan, that is. When Aunt Melinda rang the bell for lunch and the time had finally arrived to put her words into action, Jan felt shaky all over.

She followed the others into the kitchen and noticed, with relief, that Mr. Grimes hadn't come to the table yet. Now would be a good time, she decided, to slip upstairs, unnoticed.

She hurried up to the bathroom to wash her hands and lingered there until she heard Mr. Grimes' footsteps going down the stairs. When she was sure he was safely in the kitchen, she left the bathroom and fled quietly down the hall to his room.

Her heart pounding wildly, she opened his door

135

and peered inside. She stole a glance back at the empty hall, then tiptoed across the room to the dresser.

There lay the keys where she had found them yesterday. She reached out to take them, then stopped her hand in midair as troublesome thoughts raced through her head.

Can I actually go through with this? Is it really wrong to take Mr. Grimes' keys for such a short time? It really won't be stealing, she assured herself, *because I'm going to return them first thing tomorrow. Besides, he might not even miss them.*

Making up her mind to go through with her plan, Jan grasped the ring of keys and hurried from the room, closing the door softly behind her. She fled into the safety of her own room and, slipping the keys under her pillow, she left and hurried downstairs just in time to walk to the kitchen with Heather, who had been in the parlor using the phone.

"Mom said it would be all right to stay for lunch, Miss Melinda," Heather said happily.

"That's fine," Aunt Melinda said, her round face beaming. "Sit right here next to Jan.

Joey looked up when Jan took her place at the table. She smiled at him and reached for a piece of bread. He lowered his head and grinned back, knowing that she had gone through with her plan.

Mr. Grimes sipped his coffee and acted as if he didn't know the children were there. As usual he seemed preoccupied with his own thoughts. After lunch he went to his room and the children did the

136

dishes while Aunt Melinda got dressed for the festival.

"Do you think he's missed the keys yet?" Jan whispered nervously as she handed a rinsed dish to Heather to dry.

"Well, if he has, he's not making a fuss about it," Heather whispered back.

"Maybe he won't miss them at all," Joey said hopefully, reaching for the next rinsed dish.

They stopped talking when they heard Aunt Melinda coming down the stairs. While she got Bessie out of the garage and loaded her carefully wrapped pies into the trunk of the car, the children put Inky in the stable again so that he wouldn't bother Mr. Grimes if he barked. After they got the little dog settled, they climbed into the old car and were on their way.

As they drove past Mr. Grimes' Ford parked by the side of the lane, the children exchanged furtive glances, but Jan felt more guilty than the others. After all, she was responsible. The idea had been entirely hers, and she was the one who had hidden the car keys.

Aunt Melinda swung Bessie onto the road leading around the lake and Jan turned her thoughts to the festival. It would be fun helping Mr. Bronson with the ponies, she told herself, trying to put her guilty feelings out of her mind.

It was hot and stuffy in the car so they rolled down the windows. It was the hottest day of their stay at White Meadow Farm. The lake was still and glassy and the trees on the opposite shore seemed blurred in the shimmering haze.

"This is what we call threatening weather," Aunt Melinda said as she mopped her face with her handkerchief. "Not at all like our cool mountain days. It's fixing for a storm. I hope we get the festival over with before it comes."

When they arrived on the other side of the lake, they stopped at the McNeil cottage to inquire whether Heather could accompany them to the festival. Aunt Melinda told Mrs. McNeil, "It might be late when it's over, so why not let Heather spend the night with us?"

Heather squealed with delight when her parents consented. It took her only a few minutes to change into clean jeans and a blouse and to pack her overnight bag.

Mr. Bronson was waiting for them when they arrived at the festival. He told them that they were to lead the ponies around a roped-off area in the field in back of the church. Each rider was to get four turns around for twenty-five cents.

A group of noisy, anxious children had already gathered around Patches and the two brown ponies standing next to her. Mr. Bronson told the children to form a line, and Heather and the twins were kept busy with the rides until it was time to serve the covered dish supper.

"I've never seen anything like it!" exclaimed Joey when he sat down at one of the long tables in the churchyard and looked at all the good food in front of him. There were bowls of potato salad and cole slaw, fried chicken and baked ham, pickled beets and steaming roasting ears of corn. By the time the variety of pies and cakes were passed around, the

138

children were so full that they groaned with pleasure.

After the covered dish supper, Pastor Tucker spoke a few words and ended with a prayer. Then the high school band started their concert and Heather and the twins hurried back to the pony ring. Mr. Bronson relieved them now and then when they wanted to enter the cakewalk or join in the other activities that were going on. It wasn't until ten o'clock when the band stopped playing and the crowd started to thin out.

While they were helping Mr. Bronson unsaddle Patches and the ponies, a gust of wind sprang up, blowing across the church grounds, swaying the string of electric lights, and spiraling paper plates and candy wrappers through the air.

"Here comes the storm!" Mr. Bronson shouted above the rising wind. He ran for his horse van and backed it up to the pony ring. "I'd like to get the ponies in before the storm breaks," he called out. "Suppose I take Patches to my farm with the ponies and return her first thing in the morning? It'll save me a trip around the lake."

They agreed that that would be a good idea and after helping Mr. Bronson load Patches and the ponies into the van, they looked for Aunt Melinda.

She spied them first. "Get into the car," she called, her arms full of bundles she had gathered at the festival. "Hurry! Let's see if we can beat the storm."

Aunt Melinda swung Bessie around the curves in the road so fast that it made Joey think he was on a roller coaster. "You sure can drive this old thing," he shouted admirably above the noise of the engine and the wind.

Aunt Melinda laughed. "Bessie and I have been together a long time. We know each other quite well."

Flashes of lightning blinked across the dark sky, sending an eerie, green light over the lake and fields. Thunder rumbled all around them.

When one rather loud clap shook their car, Aunt Melinda said, "Don't worry. Bessie won't get struck. She has four rubber tires under her."

Just the same the mountain seemed pretty terrible with jagged forks of lightning streaking across the sky and claps of thunder cracking all around them.

By the time they drove into the lane of White Meadow Farm, the storm broke and rain was coming down in torrents. Aunt Melinda stopped the car close to the house and they scurried up the walk to the shelter of the kitchen porch.

Aunt Melinda unlocked the door and reached for the light switch. Nothing happened.

"Mercy me," she exclaimed, "lightning must have struck the power line."

They stood shivering in the darkness of the old house. Aunt Melinda closed the door and made her way across the kitchen. "I think I have some candles in the cupboard," she said. "Joey, get your flashlight so that I can find them."

Joey felt his way through the parlor. Before he reached the stairs, he stopped short, remembering that his flashlight was in the stable.

"It's in the barn," he said. "I'll run out for it."

"No you won't!" Aunt Melinda told him. "Not in this storm."

She rummaged through the contents of the cupboard. Glasses tinkled together and a cup fell to the floor and broke. "Dear me, now where did I put those candles!" she exclaimed.

The girls trembled as lightning flickered across the walls of the kitchen and thunder shook the old house.

"Where are the matches, Aunt Melinda?" Jan asked. "We could light them to see by."

"They're with the candles."

Suddenly Joey had an idea. "I could go through the tunnel for my flashlight."

"You can't find your way in the dark," Aunt Melinda told him.

"Oh, yes I can," Joey said. "I've been through that tunnel so many times, I'd know my way blindfolded. Besides, I can find my way by feeling along the sides of the wall. I'm going."

And before she could protest further, he had made his way to the cellar door and they could hear him thumping down the steps.

The girls went to the window and peered out at the storm. Lightning stabbed through the darkness and in its momentary brightness they could see the dark outlines of the old barn.

"I'll bet Inky doesn't like being out there alone," Jan remarked.

"Oh, he'll be all right," Aunt Melinda assured her. "He's used to storms." Then she added, "Maybe Mr. Grimes has a flashlight. Why didn't I think of that before?"

She made her way through the parlor to the stair landing and between rumbles of thunder they could hear her call out her boarder's name loudly. "Mr. Grimes, do you have a flashlight in your room? Mr. Grimes!"

But no answer came from the upstairs bedroom.

"I guess he went to bed early," Aunt Melinda said, returning to the kitchen, "although I can't imagine anyone being able to sleep through a storm like this one."

She began rummaging through the cupboard again. Heather turned away from the window and groped around the kitchen for a rocking chair. Jan was about to hunt for one, too, when suddenly she glimpsed a moving light in the meadow below the barn.

At first she thought it was just another flash of lightning, but as she watched, it did not flash and then go away. It was a steady light that wavered back and forth as though it were floating across the wet meadow.

"Ohhh—," she gasped in a choked voice. "It's that light again and it's coming to the barn!"

"What light?" Heather asked, leaping out of her chair and joining Jan by the window.

"The ghost light," Jan said in a small, scared voice.

She pointed with a trembling hand to the strange wavering light and felt a sudden coldness in the pit of her stomach. At this very moment Joey was making his way through the hidden tunnel to the stable!

12

THE GHOST IN THE TUNNEL

IT WAS THEN, amid a clatter of cups and saucers, that Aunt Melinda found the candles. With shaking fingers, she struck a match and lit one. The dark kitchen brightened into a soft, pale glow as she moved to the window with the flickering flame.

"Where's there a light?" she asked.

"There! There it is!" cried Heather, pointing out the window. "It's almost up to the stable."

Aunt Melinda stared through the dark pane of glass. "Landsakes, there *is* a light in the meadow!"

she exclaimed with surprise, as though she couldn't believe what she saw. "I wonder who could be out there in a night like this."

"We got to warn Joey," Jan cried. "He's in the tunnel."

Aunt Melinda stood looking at them a moment, her face grown pale in the candlelight. Then without a word she turned to the cellar door. "You girls can light another candle and wait here while I see what this is all about," she called over her shoulder.

But as Jan lit a candle she made up her mind to follow her great-aunt into the cellar. If the ghost were to confront Joey, she wanted to be nearby to help if she could. Not to be left behind alone, Heather hurried after them.

Aunt Melinda paused in front of the opening to the tunnel. She was about to call out to Joey when a strange sound from somewhere inside the tunnel made her draw back.

"What's that?" Heather asked shakily. "Is-is it the ghost?"

They held their breath and listened. There it was again, a faint, scraping sound.

Aunt Melinda's voice lowered to a whisper. "It sounds like someone digging."

A prickle of fear ran down Jan's spine. The strange noise did sound like a shovel scraping against dirt and stone. Was someone in the tunnel this very moment, digging for the treasure?

Aunt Melinda straightened her shoulders and said briskly, "We must find Joey." And without hesitating this time, she stepped forward, the dark mouth of the tunnel devouring her.

The girls trailed after her like moving shadows. The brick walls of the passageway seemed to weave mysteriously about them in the wavering candlelight and Jan felt a dizzy sensation as they crept slowly through the dark passage.

They had gone only a short distance when Aunt Melinda stopped. The girls drew close together and stared through the darkness with growing fright. Up ahead crouched a dark form. It moved suddenly and started to come toward them, casting a long shimmering shadow across the tunnel wall.

Aunt Melinda stood her ground and held up her candle. Jan was sure it was the ghost. What else could it be? She was about to let out a scream when the shadow became a familiar shape, and she let out a short gasp instead.

"Joey!"

"Shhh," cautioned the boy, putting a silencing finger to his lips. "Talk softly."

"What's going on in here?" Aunt Melinda demanded in a sharp whisper. "Who's digging in this tunnel?"

"I-I don't know," Joey said. "I've been hiding up there trying to find out. All I could see was his light shining on the tunnel walls around the turn."

"My land!" exclaimed Aunt Melinda. "Perhaps we had better go back to the house and call the state police."

But Joey shook his head. He felt braver now with all of them here. "He might get away before the police get here. Please, Aunt Melinda, this is our chance to catch him."

145

Jan felt braver, too, now that she knew Joey was safe. She whispered to her brother, "If you could see his light around the turn, he might be able to see ours."

"That's right," Joey whispered back. "You better blow out the candles."

And before Aunt Melinda could object, they drew in deep breaths and blew. The flames flickered then went out, and they were plunged once more into darkness.

"Now how can we see?" protested Aunt Melinda.

"We'll join hands and I'll lead the way," Joey suggested.

Careful not to make a sound, they proceeded slowly, feeling their way along the cold, damp bricks of the tunnel wall. When they came to the turn in the passageway, Joey stopped and Aunt Melinda and the girls peered over his shoulder. Then they, too, glimpsed the dim light glowing on the brick walls ahead.

The sound of digging had stopped. Had the intruded heard them? Was he standing in the shadows around the bend waiting for them?

Slowly Joey crept ahead again. Jan's heart pounded in her chest as they followed the light. Stealthily they rounded the turn and ahead of them the yellow glow of a lantern fell on a mound of dirt in the middle of the tunnel. A dark shape bending over the mound seemed to be the figure of a boy.

The Indian boy jumped to get away, but Joey reached out and grabbed his arm. "So it was you who was digging in the tunnel," he said.

146

They were all so surprised that they stood like statues, staring wordlessly at the familiar intruder. It was Aunt Melinda, who found her voice first.

"Jim Eagle!" she called out sharply. "What are you doing in my tunnel this time of night?"

The Indian boy swung around with surprise, his startled face pale in the glow of the lantern. Like a taut spring he jumped to get away, but Joey reached out and grabbed his arm.

"So it was you who was digging in the tunnel!" he said, accusingly.

The boy shook his head and pointed back through the darkness. "It wasn't me—it was him!"

"Who, Jim?" asked Aunt Melinda.

The boy shook himself free from Joey's grasp and shrugged his thin shoulders. "I don't know. It was some man I never saw before. I was in the stable and when I heard someone digging in the tunnel, I came through to find out what was going on. Then I saw him. I guess I must have scared him because he went out that way. Back toward the stable."

"Was he medium height and did he have a high forehead and light brown hair?" Jan asked breathlessly.

Jim nodded, and the children looked at one another with knowing glances.

"Mr. Grimes!" breathed Joey.

"Now we don't know for sure," Aunt Melinda cautioned. She turned to Jim Eagle. "Why were you in the stable tonight, Jim?"

The Indian boy hung his head and remained silent.

"Where is your uncle?" Aunt Melinda prompted.

148

"I thought he was coming for you. Weren't you to go back with him to New Mexico while your father is in the hospital?"

Jim Eagle sank against the wall of the tunnel like a cornered animal. He wasn't angry nor defiant now. He seemed frightened and tired. Jan almost felt sorry for him.

"It's because of my uncle that I'm here, Miss Melinda," he managed to say in a low voice. "But I didn't mean no harm. Honest."

Aunt Melinda said gently, "Well, suppose you tell us all about it and there's no better time than the present."

Jim was silent for a moment, then he drew in a long shaky breath and blurted out the story. "I don't want to go to New Mexico to live with my uncle. It's not because I don't like him, but I want to stay here until Pa gets well. I don't want to leave him. Pa and I have always been together. I was afraid if I stayed at our house, Uncle Red Cloud would find me there and take me away; so I decided to hide on the island. When it rained, I'd come over here and stay in the barn to keep dry."

"Then it was your light we saw tonight in the meadow!" cried Jan.

The boy nodded and looked down at his bare feet which were working about in the pile of loose dirt. "I kept an old blanket here in the barn. You don't use the haymow anymore, Miss Melinda, so I didn't think it'd matter if I slept in the hay."

"The haymow!" Joey broke in. "Then it must have been your footsteps we heard in the barn the first day we were here."

149

Again the boy nodded. "When I heard you and your sister playing in the loft that day, I hid in the tunnel. Pa told me about the tunnel and how it was used by runaway slaves in the old days. I found the trapdoor underneath the bale of straw in the stable and thought I could hide there, like the slaves did, if anybody came hunting for me."

"Well, I never!" exclaimed Aunt Melinda. And before anyone could say anything more, Joey confronted Jim Eagle with another question.

"Then you don't really believe Aunt Melinda's barn is haunted?"

Jim smiled for the first time. "No, I just told you that so you'd stay away from the barn and wouldn't catch me hiding here."

Aunt Melinda put her hand on Jim's shoulder and looked sympathetic. "But how can you stay alone without your father? What do you eat?"

Jim drew himself up proudly. "Oh, I can take care of myself, Miss Melinda," he said, "and I get enough to eat. I fish and pick apples and berries and Pa left me a little money to spend for milk and stuff. Sometimes I catch enough fish to sell to the restaurant at the motel."

As she listened to what Jim Eagle was telling them, Jan was so excited that she kept hopping on one foot and then on the other. "You sure are solving our mysteries for us, Jim," she said.

"Yeah," her brother agreed, "now we know whose footsteps we heard in the loft and the mystery of the spooky light in the meadow on stormy nights."

"What about Miss Melinda's missing pie?" Heather suddenly remembered.

The Indian boy looked funny, as if he didn't want to talk about that. But he knew he had to; so taking a long breath, he said, "I was in the tunnel the day you kids brought the hammer in and started tapping the sides of the walls. I couldn't figure out what you were doing, but when I heard you coming on through the tunnel, I hid in the fruit cellar. It was then that I saw the two pies."

He turned to Aunt Melinda, then hanging his head, he confessed in a low voice, "I was so hungry that day, I took one of them. I was hoping you wouldn't miss it. I took it to the island and had it for supper that night. But after I ate it, I felt sorry I took it and then when I saw you all on the island the next day, I got real mad."

Aunt Melinda surprised him by laughing gaily. "I guess we were the last people on earth you wanted to meet after you had eaten the pie." She added kindly, "I understand. You were welcome to that pie, Jim. Now let's get out of this damp tunnel and go up to the kitchen. I brought a chocolate cake home from the festival and I know that will taste just as good as blueberry pie."

Jim's eyes lighted up at the mention of chocolate cake. Picking up his lantern, he willingly followed the others back through the dark tunnel.

13

THE SECRET ROOM

THEY WERE surprised to find a light in the kitchen when they climbed the cellar steps. Propped on the table was the largest flashlight they had ever seen. They were even more surprised to find somebody was sitting at the kitchen table waiting for them. It was Mr. Grimes.

The children stepped into the kitchen and stared at the man. By the appearance of his wet hair and soggy jacket he had just come in from the storm outside. He hadn't been asleep in his room at all as

Aunt Melinda had thought. He glanced up at them and an uneasy, guilty look came over his face.

Aunt Melinda hustled over to the table where she had left her bundles from the festival. "We were just going to have some refreshments and you must join us," she told her boarder as if she weren't at all surprised to find him sitting there, damp from the rain.

But before she could say anything further, Mr. Grimes declared in his usual solemn voice, "I am here not to eat but to make a confession, Miss Howard." Pointing to Jim Eagle, he said, "This boy probably told you that he saw me in the tunnel."

Jim gasped and stepped back from the pointing finger. When he caught his breath, he cried out, "That's the man I saw, Miss Melinda!"

"Why, mercy, Mr. Grimes, what in the world were you doing in the tunnel on a night like this?"

"I have been digging there," Mr. Grimes stated flatly. "I have been hunting for a chest of gold, half of which rightfully belonged to my great-great-grandfather."

At these words Aunt Melinda couldn't hide her surprise any longer. Her jaw dropped and she stared at the man as if she could not believe what she had heard him say.

"Then you must be a descendant of Henry Sterret!"

"Yes, he was my great-great-grandfather," replied Mr. Grimes.

Aunt Melinda pulled a chair from the table and sat down next to her boarder. Her eyes were dancing with excitement. "All these years my family has been wondering what happened to the Sterrets after they had left here," she said. "You must tell us all about them."

Eager to learn what had happened to the man who had helped John Howard hide the lost treasure in the tunnel and then had disappeared so mysteriously, the children joined Aunt Melinda at the table. They all looked expectantly at Mr. Grimes.

The boarder leaned back in his chair and cleared his throat. "Well," he began, "my great-great-grandfather left here for Massachusetts with his son Nathan and his family. Having failed as a farmer, Nathan decided to move to Boston to try his fortune at sea. He got a job as a hand on a whaler, the *Molly O*, but on his first voyage out, the ship sank at sea in a hurricane."

Heather's breath caught in a soft gasp. "How awful!"

Mr. Grimes nodded slowly several times. His voice grew even more solemn as he continued. "You can imagine the terrible time my great-grandmother had after that with five children to feed and take care of. She remembered something that Nathan, her husband, had told her about some gold his father, Henry Sterret, and John Howard had hidden at White Meadow Farm in Pennsylvania. But when she asked her father-in-law about it, he couldn't tell her. You see, the shock of losing his only son at sea had been too much for the old man and his mind went blank. He couldn't remember a thing about the treasure and at the end he didn't even know his own name."

Mr. Grimes paused a minute, while they waited

154

in sympathetic silence. Never had he said so much at one time before nor had he had such an attentive audience.

"Both Henry Sterret and my great-grandmother died shortly after Nathan was lost at sea," he continued, " and my great-grandmother never had the chance to return to Pennsylvania to see about the treasure. With no parents left to care for them, Nathan's five children left Boston and went to live with relatives."

"So that's why folks around here lost touch with the Sterrets," Aunt Melinda said, shaking her head sadly.

Mr. Grimes nodded. "Yes, it was because all five children were scattered among the relatives and grew up in different places. They were too young to remember much about the treasure, so it was forgotten until last year when my own mother died. After her death, while I was going through some old family papers, I discovered my great-grandmother's copybook in which there was an entry telling about the chest of gold."

Mr. Grimes took a bite of cake which Aunt Melinda had placed before him. While he had been talking, she had cut the chocolate cake into six generous pieces.

"Well," he went on, "I kept wondering about that missing gold. Nobody else in the family seemed to know anything about it. But the possibility that Great-Great-Grandfather Sterret might have left a treasure behind at White Meadow Farm never left my mind. So I decided to come here and see if I could locate it.

"I found Martha Howard's diary in the bookcase the day you said I could read any one of those books there. That told me that the gold had been kept in the hidden tunnel. I found the tunnel the day you picnicked on the island and decided to hunt for the treasure."

"So that's why you wanted to rent a room at White Meadow Farm!" Jan broke in.

"Yes, that was my main reason," Mr. Grimes admitted. He looked squarely at Aunt Melinda. "If I had found the treasure, I would have taken what belonged to my family and would have given the rest to you, Miss Howard. But I didn't find it."

Aunt Melinda looked puzzled. "Why didn't you tell me about wanting to hunt for Henry Sterret's share of the treasure?" she questioned. "I could have told you more about it."

Mr. Grimes looked apologetic. "I didn't know whether you knew about the treasure or not. And then, the children—I certainly didn't want word of it to get out to anyone else. You know what would have happened, Miss Howard. White Meadow Farm would have been filled with treasure seekers."

Jan sighed and glanced at her brother and Heather. Why did grown-ups seem to think that kids couldn't be confided in? Why, kids could keep secrets just as well as anybody else—sometimes even better!

"But the children do know," Aunt Melinda was telling him. "All our family has known about the chest of gold ever since John Howard and Henry Sterret hid it in the tunnel. Like your great-great-

156

grandfather, John Howard died before he could tell anyone just where in the tunnel the treasure was hidden. For generations we Howards have been hunting for it. The tunnel has been searched again and again. It's strange that the treasure has never been found."

Mr. Grimes shook his head regretfully. "Yes, it's certainly strange."

He seemed so disappointed that Jan couldn't help feeling sorry for him. After all, half of the gold did rightfully belong to his family and maybe they needed their share of it as much as Aunt Melinda needed hers.

She stared down at her empty cake plate for a long moment and frowned thoughtfully. Where in the tunnel could the chest of gold be hidden? she wondered. As Aunt Melinda had said, it was strange that after so many years and with so many Howards hunting for it, it hadn't been found. It would almost seem as if the treasure weren't hidden in the tunnel at all!

This new possibility struck Jan like a blow. As she thought about it, her frown changed to a smile that grew until her whole face was beaming.

"Maybe that treasure isn't in the hidden tunnel as everybody thought it was," she spoke her thoughts aloud.

They all looked at her with amazed silence. Then Aunt Melinda spoke.

"Why, what do you mean by that, child?"

"Martha Howard's diary said it was there,"Joey reminded her.

"But maybe John Howard moved it for some

157

reason," Jan went on to explain, "and Martha Howard didn't know about it."

"Well, if it isn't in the hidden tunnel, I wouldn't know where else to look for it," Aunt Melinda said. "There's not another hiding place on the farm."

"Oh, yes there is!" cried Jan.

Aunt Melinda looked sharply at her great-niece. "Do you mean the secret room in the attic?"

Jan nodded. "The room where the runaway slaves were hidden."

For a moment nobody spoke. Then Mr. Grimes looked over at Jan with an unexpected smile that showed he shared her excitement. "Maybe Jan has something there," he told the others.

His mood was catching and now they were all excited over Jan's idea. Joey threw his sister a look of admiration and Heather blinked happily at her friend. Jim Eagle's dark eyes sparkled with excitement as he sat quietly listening.

Mr. Grimes turned to Aunt Melinda. "I'd like to see that room, Miss Howard. I've often heard about those hidden rooms built in false walls of old houses. I'm a carpenter by trade and if you don't mind, I'd like to have a look."

"We'll all have a look," Aunt Melinda said, "but we'll have to wait until tomorrow. With no lights, we can't go up there tonight."

Mr. Grimes nodded agreement and consulted his watch. "Isn't it getting late for you young folks? I know it's time for me to turn in."

"Aw, shucks," groaned Joey, but when Aunt Melinda told him that Jim Eagle could sleep with him that night, he brightened and rushed upstairs ahead of the others to show the Indian boy his room.

Across the hall in Jan's room the girls lay awake talking. With everything that had happened that evening, their minds buzzed with excitement and sleep seemed far off. But at last they fell silent as did the boys across the way and the old farmhouse was quiet once more. Only the grandfather clock on the landing below spoke out the hours in deep tones throughout the rest of the night.

Aunt Melinda's bell awoke them the next morning. The children dressed quickly and went downstairs. Mr. Grimes was already at the kitchen table, warming his hands around a cup of coffee. To their surprise he smiled as they took their places at the table and was as talkative during breakfast as he had been the night before. He seemed like a different person today.

It's because he has nothing to hide from us anymore, Jan thought happily. *He's not going to hunt for the treasure secretly and all by himself, but he's going to help us look for it today.*

Jim Eagle seemed different, too. Now that he had friends with whom to share his troubles, he wasn't scowling this morning. The smile that brightened his thin, brown face told her that he wanted to be their friend, too.

After breakfast Aunt Melinda stacked the dishes and they all followed her up the circular stairs to the attic. She led the way past the old trunks and furniture to the south wall where she pressed the middle panel of the false wall and the spring

159

released the hidden opening.

"Well, I'll be!" exclaimed Mr. Grimes, his sharp gray eyes seeming to pop from his head as he peered into the opening in the wall.

Jim Eagle's dark eyes sparkled with excitement. "Oh, boy, wait till I tell Pa that I saw the Howards' secret room!" he cried.

While the others crowded inside the small room, Mr. Grimes carefully examined the false wall. He ran his hand over the opening in the wood and remarked, "I've never seen anything like this before. Whoever built this secret room, Miss Howard, was a fine craftsman."

"John Howard designed it himself," Aunt Melinda spoke with pride.

Meanwhile the children were busy searching the room. They examined every inch of the walls and each floorboard that might reveal a hiding place for the treasure. They even searched through the trunk of old clothes to the very bottom.

"Well, there doesn't seem to be any treasure here," Jan said with a sigh as she and Heather piled the clothes back into the trunk.

"There's no treasure under here, either," said Jim Eagle, who had been on his hands and knees, looking underneath the cot.

Jan sank back on her knees besides the trunk. "Maybe my idea wasn't so hot after all," she moaned.

"Oh, it was a good idea, Jan," Heather said loyally. "We just have to keep on looking."

While they continued their search, Joey walked over to the back wall and examined it again. "Why was this end of the secret room built into the chimney?" he wanted to know.

"It was a way to keep this little room warm in the winter," Aunt Melinda explained. "There was always a fire in the fireplaces below; it was the only way to heat the house in those days. That's why this old cot was pushed up against the chimney. It made a snug bed during cold winter nights when the runaway slaves occupied this part of the attic."

"Hmm," Mr. Grimes murmured, taking a sudden interest in the chimney. He walked over to it and examined the wall behind the cot. Then he stepped out of the room and measured the width of the chimney with his arms. Without a word, he opened one of the small attic windows and peered at the outside of the chimney. The others were puzzled as they watched him.

"I'd like to measure the chimney on the outside," Mr. Grimes explained. "Does anybody have a yardstick or a straight piece of wood?"

Aunt Melinda rummaged through an old box in another part of the attic and found a yardstick.

"What a queer thing to do," Heather whispered to Jan.

"He seems more interested in how this old room was built than helping us hunt for the treasure," Jan whispered back with disappointment.

Mr. Grimes leaned out of the window as far as he could and placed the yardstick along the outside of the chimney. "I can't reach all the way across it but I have a pretty fair idea how wide it is," he called back to them.

He drew himself back inside the window and

began to measure the chimney from the inside. A pleased expression appeared on his face as he read the yardstick.

"Just as I thought," he said softly, as if he were thinking out loud. "The chimney here, outside the secret room, seems to be the same width as it is on the outside of the house."

"It would be, wouldn't it?" Jan said, growing impatient with his elaborate calculations.

Mr. Grimes shook his head. "No, it shouldn't be the same. It should be more narrow here, considering that part of the inside chimney extends into the secret room."

Jan shook her head in bewilderment. She couldn't understand what Mr. Grimes was talking about. But, then, she had always been terrible in math.

Joey seemed to understand. "I get it!" he cried. "That means that the chimney inside here was enlarged."

"That's right, son," Mr. Grimes said. "You have a good head on your shoulders. Now why would John Howard want to enlarge the part of the chimney inside the secret room when he could have built the secret room against the chimney as it was? There must be another reason than just to warm the persons sleeping there."

Joey was really excited now as he followed Mr. Grimes back into the little room. The others trailed after them. Mr. Grimes pulled the cot out of the way and bent over to examine the bricks at the base of the chimney. They all crowded around to watch.

The chimney looked the same here to Jan as it did

on the outside--just ordinary bricks. She was puzzled as she watched Mr. Grimes run his fingers down along the mortar between each brick. It was then that she noticed there was no mortar between the bricks behind the cot.

Mr. Grimes tapped them and tried to wiggle them loose, but they seemed to stick.

"I'll need a hammer and chisel," he said.

Joey leaped up. "I'll get them in the toolshed." He flew down the attic steps and was back in no time, with Inky at his heels.

The boys held the chisel while Mr. Grimes tapped it gently with the hammer. Finally the bricks wiggled loose.

"Now see if you can pull them out," Mr. Grimes told the boys.

Joey and Jim reached for the bricks and drew them out one by one until a dark opening in the base of the chimney gaped at them.

"Is there anything in there?" Aunt Melinda asked breathleooly.

Jim Eagle got down on his hands and knees and peered into the opening. "It's too dark to see."

"I brought my flashlight from the barn when I went for the hammer and chisel," Joey said, reaching into his back pocket.

Anxiously they gathered around him as he flicked on the light and beamed it over the double rows of bricks in the two inner walls and along the top and bottom of the opening. Jan's heart fell as she squinted into the dark space that seemed to be empty.

"Give me that flashlight," said Mr. Grimes.

Joey handed it to him and Mr. Grimes extended the flashlight into the opening as far as his arm could reach and aimed the beam directly at the back wall.

At once everyone drew in his breath. There, way back in the hidden recess in the chimney, the brass fastenings of a metal chest blinked out at them.

14

THE LOST TREASURE

THEY WERE all so surprised that for a long moment they just stood there staring in awed silence at the chest. Then Aunt Melinda, her voice trembling with excitement, said, "Well, isn't anyone going to pull it out and see what's in it?"

With that they sprang into action. Joey held the light while Mr. Grimes reached into the chimney. "We'll have to make the hole a little bigger," he told the boys. "It's so far back, I can't reach it."

With hammer and chisel they removed several

more bricks, then Mr. Grimes thrust both his arm and shoulder far back into the opening and pulled out the chest.

"Let's take it to the window where we can see better." Aunt Melinda suggested.

With the boys' help Mr. Grimes carried the heavy chest out of the secret room and placed it in front of the open window where the sun poured in and blazed on the brass lock.

Mr. Grimes stood up and brushed the dust from his hands. "You open it, Miss Howard. After all, it was found in your attic."

With trembling fingers, Aunt Melinda tried the clasp that held the lid shut. But the clasp wouldn't open. Mr. Grimes bent over to examine the lock.

"We'll need a key," he said.

"I'll see if there's one in the chimney," Joey offered, springing to his feet. Jim Eagle followed him back into the secret room.

While Jim held the flashlight, Joey peered inside the gaping hole in the chimney. He felt around in the dark corners and ran his fingers up along the bricks and across the bottom of the opening, but couldn't find the key.

"John Howard must have kept the key somewhere else," he announced when he and Jim emerged from the secret room.

"But we'll never know what's in the chest if we can't get it open," wailed Jan.

"We can try to break it open," Joey suggested.

"Oh, no. I wouldn't want such a valuable old chest broken open," Aunt Melinda said quickly.

All this time Mr. Grimes had been quietly examing the brass lock. "I think I can get it open. I have taken many locks off doors and chests and replaced them with new ones. After we get the chest open, Miss Howard, I'll put the lock back on again. Then you can get a locksmith to make a new key for it."

Aunt Melinda's eyes sparkled. "Why, that would be just dandy."

"I'll need some tools," Mr. Grimes said. "I have a tool case in the trunk of my car. I'll get it and work on this chest right away."

He rose and went down the attic steps. While they waited for him, they sat around the mysterious chest and tried to imagine what was inside.

"I hope it's filled with gold," said Jan, dreamily.

"It's heavy enough for gold," Joey told her.

"Oh, it must be the lost treasure!" Heather exclaimed excitedly.

"We'll soon find out," Aunt Melinda told them, her cheeks flushed with anticipation.

They waited for what seemed to be hours. Jim Eagle wiggled around impatiently. "What's taking that guy so long? It shouldn't take him this long to get his car keys and go out there and open up his trunk."

At the mention of the words *car keys*, the twins and Heather looked at one another, horrified.

"Oh!" gasped Jan, clapping her hand over her mouth. In the excitement of searching the secret room, she had forgotten all about returning Mr. Grimes' keys that morning.

"What's the matter?" Aunt Melinda asked, noticing the startled expressions on their faces.

"He—he's probably hunting for his keys," Jan

167

murmured in a small voice. A wave of shame swept over her and she could feel her cheeks growing hot. There was nothing to do but to tell Aunt Melinda what she had done.

After listening to Jan's story, Aunt Melinda didn't scold, but her face had a disapproving look. "I suggest you go right down to your room, Jan, and get those keys for Mr. Grimes. You'll have to explain to him why you took them. Now hurry, the poor man is probably hunting all over for them."

Jan fled across the attic floor and down the circular stairs. Joey hurried after her. He was in this as much as she and it wouldn't be right to let her face Mr. Grimes alone.

They got the ring of keys from Jan's room—it was still under her pillow—and moved hesitantly toward Mr. Grimes' room. The door was open and they found him on his hands and knees, looking under the bottom of the dresser.

"Oh, drat it! Now where did those keys get to?" he was muttering to himself.

"Here they are, Mr. Grimes," Jan said in a thin, shaky voice as she held the keys out to him.

The man rose to his feet and stared at her with his sharp gray eyes. "Where did you find them?"

"I-I took them," Jan said falteringly. Then, with Joey's help, she poured out her confession.

To their surprise Mr. Grimes just laughed after he had heard their story. "Well, come to think of it, I can't blame you for hiding my keys. I guess I did act mighty suspicious yesterday, taking that diary and digging in the tunnel. Hiding my keys sort of evens things up, I'd say."

168

As he spoke, he reached for Martha Howard's diary on top of the dresser and handed it to Jan in exchange for the keys.

"Now come on. We have to get my tools and see what's in that chest."

The twins were so relieved that Mr. Grimes wasn't angry that they tore out of the room and down the stairs on the run to help get the tool case.

"I carry it around with me wherever I go, just like the doctor carries around his little black bag," Mr. Grimes told them after he unlocked the trunk of his car and brought out the case. "Never know when my tools will come in handy."

The three of them hurried back to the attic where the others were waiting anxiously. Mr. Grimes opened his tool case, chose several small tools, and went to work on the lock. In no time he had it loose. It made a funny little clicking sound as he took it off the chest.

"Now this lid will open," he said triumphantly, laying the lock aside.

Inky gave a sharp bark and wagged his tail expectantly as Aunt Melinda placed her hand on the lid. Jan bit her lip. It was a breathless, exciting moment.

At last the chest was open and the glow of the sun shining through the little attic window matched the soft glow of the gold coins that lay in neat rows before them.

A hush settled over the attic as they all stared at the treasure that had been placed in this chest so many years ago. It was as if the sight of the missing gold coins had cast a spell on the six eager faces that peered down at them. Nobody had words to speak for the moment.

It was Aunt Melinda, who broke the spell. "My goodness!" she breathed. "My goodness!" Then she seemed to forget all the others as she wiped the tears of happiness from her eyes and sat back, blinking at the chest of gold.

Jan reached into the chest and pulled out a piece of paper, brown with age.

"Look, Aunt Melinda, here's a note," she said curiously, handing the paper to her great-aunt.

With trembling hands, Aunt Melinda took the note and peered down at the faded words written on it.

"What does it say?" Joey asked. He could hardly stand the suspense.

"Read it," they all chorused.

Aunt Melinda wiped her eyes and straightened her shoulders to compose herself. "There's a date on the paper," she told them. "June 29, 1902." Then she read the note slowly, for it was difficult to make out the flowing, old-fashioned script. " 'On this day Henry Sterret and his son, Nathan, and family moved away. Henry asked me to keep his share of the gold with mine until he got settled in Boston. Since I am now responsible for his share, I thought it would be better to move the chest from the hidden tunnel and keep it here in the house, in the chimney of the secret room where the runaways used to hide their belongings. You all know about

Mr. Grimes opened his tool case, chose several small tools, and went to work on the lock. In no time he had it loose.

170

this hiding place in the chimney; so, if anything happens to me, I'm sure that when you don't find the gold in the tunnel, you'll look for it in the secret room. It will be safer here because too many people have found out about the tunnel under our farm.' "

"There's initials at the bottom of the note," Jan observed, looking over her great-aunt's shoulder. "The initials are J.H."

"John Howard," breathed Aunt Melinda. "Now we know why the chest of gold was never found in the hidden tunnel."

Joey's voice was suddenly thoughtful. "If Martha Howard's family knew about this hiding place in the chimney, why didn't they look here for the treasure when they couldn't find it in the tunnel?"

"I guess we'll never know why they didn't find the treasure here, Joey," Aunt Melinda said, shaking her head.

"We wouldn't have found it here, either, if it hadn't been for Miss Jan's idea to search the secret room," Mr. Grimes added, winking over at her.

All at once Jan had a warm feeling for the mysterious Mr. Grimes. His wink told her again that he had forgiven her for taking his keys—that they had been conspirators together in hunting the treasure. It was good to know how different people could be after you really got to know them.

"And it was your knowledge of carpentry that led us to search in the chimney," Aunt Melinda added, with praise for her boarder. "Without you and the children, I would never have found this treasure."

Mr. Grimes' smile widened as he stared down at the gold coins.

"Why, there's enough treasure here for both of us, Miss Howard," he said happily.

"I'll call James Larson from the bank right away," Aunt Melinda said. "He'll know what to do about exchanging this gold for money we can use."

The children bent over to touch the coins. They would probably never have the chance to touch so much gold at one time again.

Joey flopped down on the floor next to the chest. "Until Mr. Larson gets here, I'm not leaving this gold out of my sight for a minute," he said.

"I'll stay here with you and help you guard it," Jim Eagle volunteered.

"Ruff!" Inky wagged his tail, telling them he would be their watchdog.

Just then, from the open window, they heard the crunch of tires on the lane outside.

"There's Mr. Bronson," Heather said as she looked down at the red and white horse van coming to a stop by the stable door. In all the excitement of finding the gold, they had forgotten about Mr. Bronson's promise to bring Patches home that morning.

The girls hurried down the attic stairs with Aunt Melinda, and while she telephoned Mr. Larson, they ran outside to help Mr. Bronson with Patches.

As they crossed the yard toward the stable, Jan said, "Oh, Heather, isn't it wonderful! Now Aunt Melinda will be able to keep White Meadow Farm."

"And you and Joey will be able to come back to White Meadow Lake again next year," Heather added, giving her friend's hand a little squeeze of happiness.

By the time the girls had fed Patches her oats and had turned her out to pasture, Mr. Larson's sleek black car had turned into the lane.

Aunt Melinda led the banker into the attic where Mr. Grimes and the boys were still guarding the chest of gold. She introduced the two men and explained that half of the gold coins belonged to Mr. Grimes.

The men shook hands and Mr. Larson said, "Come back to the bank with me, sir, and after you are properly identified, we'll see that you get your share. Then we shall exchange this gold for legal currency."

The banker bent over the chest to examine the coins. "They are all golden eagles," he told them. "Ten dollar gold pieces. But each piece is worth more than one hundred dollars now."

Joey whistled through his teeth and Jan exclaimed, "Wow-wee!"

Mr. Larson was silent for several long minutes while he counted the rows. "There are five hundred pieces here," he said at last.

Joey spoke up, "Will half of them be enough to pay Aunt Melinda's mortgage?"

Mr. Larson smiled. "Yes, more than enough. There will be enough left over to turn White Meadow Farm into the most up-to-date guesthouse on the lake, if your great-aunt would want to do that."

"What a wonderful idea, James!" Aunt Melinda exclaimed. "That's just what I will do. Then I'll always have a way to make a living right here on my farm.

174

"Of course," she added, gathering Jan and Joey close to her and hugging them, "you two will always be my most cherished guests, even if you did find out about my secret of the mortgage."

"I didn't mean to eavesdrop that day," Joey said, his face getting very red.

Aunt Melinda gave him an affectionate squeeze. "It doesn't matter. I'm glad now that you did. It made you more determined than ever to find this treasure."

While the others were beaming with happiness, there was a little shadow of worry in Heather's hazel eyes. "If you are going to change White Meadow Farm into a guesthouse, Miss Melinda, can Patches still stay in your barn?"

"Mercy, yes, child. After all, Patches is the first boarder I have ever had and I wouldn't think of not giving her a place to stay."

"You know, Miss Howard," Mr. Grimes spoke up with a thoughtful grin, "I wouldn't mind coming back here, myself, next summer. I've taken quite a fancy to the place. Would you reserve a room for me, too?"

Aunt Melinda flashed her boarder an understanding smile. "Of course I will. You can have the very same room you have now."

"Do you really like to go fishing?" Joey asked.

Mr. Grimes threw back his head and laughed. "Yes, boy, I really do. More than digging in tunnels! Maybe you'd like to go with me sometime."

"Boy, I sure would," Joey replied eagerly.

Aunt Melinda turned her attention to Jim Eagle. "Now, Jim," she said, "if I'm going to run a

175

guesthouse, I'll need a good handyman around. Do you think you'd like the job?"

"You bet I would!" the Indian boy exclaimed.

"Well, you can start right now if you like," Aunt Melinda told him. "There's plenty of work to be done, cutting the grass and trimming the bushes. Tomorrow, I'll visit your father in the hospital and tell him that you don't have to go to the reservation with your uncle. You can stay right here at White Meadow Farm with me until your father gets out of the hospital."

"Whoopee!" Jim Eagle shouted, looking happier than any boy Jan had ever seen. "I'll get started on that grass right away," he promised when he caught his breath.

"I'll help you," offered Joey. "Then maybe later on we can go fishing."

In smiling silence, Jan watched her brother and Jim go arm in arm down the attic steps. Now she knew what Aunt Melinda had meant when she had told them that if a boy acted the way Jim Eagle had acted, there must be a reason for it, and that they should look for that reason with kindness and understanding.

Jan turned back to the chest of gold coins with a happy sigh. They really found something when they found that treasure, but she couldn't help thinking that they had discovered something even more important than gold.

Her great-aunt put her silent thought into words when she told Mr. Larson, "Didn't I tell you, James, that nothing is impossible when you put your trust in the Lord?"

The banker nodded and smiled. "Yes, you did, Melinda. It's certainly remarkable how things have worked out for you."

The men carried the heavy chest down the attic stairs and out of the house to Mr. Larson's car. Aunt Melinda and the girls followed.

Linking her arm through Heather's, Jan said happily, "While Aunt Melinda and Mr. Grimes take the gold to the bank, let's ride Patches. After all, we haven't seen much of her since last night and we certainly do have a lot to tell her."

David Klucsik, *Allentown Call-Chronicle*

Ruth Nulton Moore likes to write books packed full of adventure, whether they be historical novels or mysteries. *Mystery of the Lost Treasure* takes place in the Pocono Mountains of Pennsylvania, near where she lives.

Mrs. Moore was born in Easton, Pennsylvania, and now lives in Bethlehem, Pennsylvania, with her husband, a professor of accounting at Lehigh University. They have two sons in college.

A former public school teacher, she has written poetry and stories for *Children's Activities* and *Jack and Jill.* One of her stories has been adapted in an elementary school reader *(High and Wide,* Book 3-1, American Book Company, 1968) and in several reading workbooks. She is author of *Frisky, the Playful Pony,* published by Criterion and translated into Swedish by Walstroms Bokforlag, *Hiding the Bell* (Westminster Press), *Peace Treaty* and *The Ghost Bird Mystery* (Herald Press).

Mrs. Moore likes to combine fictional adventure with a Christian message for the 9-to-14-age-group.